Walking Wolf

A WEIRD WESTERN
NANCY A. COLLINS

MARK V. ZIESING
SHINGLETOWN, CA
1995

Published by
Mark V. Ziesing
Post Office Box 76
Shingletown, CA 96088

Manufactured in the
United States of America

FIRST EDITION

*Dustjacket Design, Hand Lettering and
Book Design* by Arnie Fenner
Production Design by Robert Frazier

SIGNED LIMITED EDITION:
ISBN 0-929480-43-0
TRADE EDITION:
ISBN 0-929480-42-2
LIBRARY OF CONGRESS:
95-060176

This one's for
Joe R. Lansdale, Clint Eastwood,
Sam Peckinpah, Jonah Hex,
Thomas Berger, El Topo
and everyone else who ever
held the Old West
by its bootheels and shook it
for all it was worth

The following books were valuable sources of information concerning the lifestyles and belief systems of the North American Plains Indians: *The Dictionary of the American Indian* by John Stoutenburgh, Jr.; *The Mythology of North America* by John Bierhorst, *The Comanches: Lords of the South Plains* by Wallace & Hoebel; *The Indian Frontier of the American West 1846-1890* by Robert M. Utley; *Plains Indians Mythology* by Marriott & Rachlin; *The Indians of Texas* by W.W. Newcomb, Jr.; *The Encyclopedia of Frontier Biography, Vol.1-3* by Dan L. Thrapp, *Ghost Dance* by David Humphreys Miller; *Comanche Moon* by Jack Jackson; and *Freak Show: Presenting Human Oddities for Amusement and Profit* by Robert Bogdan.

Walking Wolf

PROLOGUE

Every kid plays at cowboys and indians, sometime or another, no matter what their sex, race, background or temperament. I was no different—except I wasn't playing. It was how I lived.

My name is William Skillet. That's my White name. My Indian name—some would say it was my *real* name—is Walking Wolf. I was raised by the Comanche as one of their own on the open plains of what are now the states of New Mexico, Oklahoma, and Texas.

Now I know what you're thinking. I can't be more than fifty years old, by the looks of me. And the last time the Comanche lived free of the reservations was before the turn of the Twentieth century, which would make me either quite well-preserved or a damn liar.

Well, I have been known to lie on occasion, but this time I'm giving you the straight skinny. To the best of my knowledge, I'm one hundred and fifty, give or take a year. The reason I'm vague as to my exact age is that I don't really know when I was born. Eight Clouds Rising— my adopted father—could only tell me that he found me during the season the buffalo cows dropped their calves, the year after the smallpox went through the tribe, claiming the life of his only natural son. Which probably means I was born sometime in 1844.

But I *can* tell you the reason for me being so youthful-looking for a man a century and a half old. I'm not exactly what you'd call human. Hell, I'm not human at all. The closest thing you might be able to relate me to is what's known as a "werewolf", but not the kind you see in the picture shows that sprout hair and teeth every time there's a full moon. The truth of my kind is a lot more complicated—and frightening—than that.

What your about to read is the story of my life—leastwise, the early part of it. I wrote it more for my sake than anything else. As I've gotten older, the past has a tendency to be both fuzzy and painfully distinct. Sometimes when I get up in the morning, I'm surprised to find myself in a house, not a *tipi*. And when I look out the picture window, I almost expect to see a herd of buffalo grazing in the valley below. Other times, I find myself grasping for the name of a loved one like it was a bubble in a stream. I do not want to forget that time, to lose it the truth under the weight of a new century's memories.

Now I don't want anyone reading this to think I'm bragging about having lead an interesting life. Life ain't nothing more than the things that happen to you on your way to dying. Some folks just have more things happen to 'em, and in an entertaining fashion, than others, that's all.

I guess I've said all that needs to be said in the way of an explanation, except that anyone attempting to find a moral will be gut-shot.

CHAPTER ONE

I don't remember my real family. And although I've had all kinds of names in my lifetime, both Indian and White—I don't know the name my flesh-and-blood folks gave me when I was born.

All I know about my ma is that she was human, probably from the Old Country. My pa was a *vargr* (that's what werewolves call themselves) who went by the name of Howler. And for some reason, in the early 1840s they moved out into the wilderness surrounding what would eventually become Dallas, Texas.

My story begins with a Comanche brave of the name Eight Clouds Rising coming home after a successful attempt at stealing Apache ponies. Eight Clouds belonged to the *Penatekas* band, who were famed for their lightning-fast raids, hence their nickname of "Wasp Riders." As he made his way back to his camp, he caught sight of a thin spume of smoke on the horizon. Then he spied the buzzards. Eight Clouds, being inquisitive by nature, decided to check it out.

The cabin was still smoldering when he arrived. To hear him tell it, he'd been surprised to see a White homestead so close to Comanche territory. Whites preferred being within a half-day's ride of one another, yet the nearest White settlement had to be a good three days' journey from there. As he drew closer the ponies rolled their eyes and whinnied at the stink of death hanging thick in the air.

There was a body sprawled before the collapsed ruin of the two-room cabin. The corpse was that of a boy of nine or ten—the same age as his own son, Little Eagle, who'd died last spring. The boy was dressed in a rough-woven flaxen shirt and crude canvas overalls, his feet bare and tough as leather. He'd been shot in the chest and his throat slit from ear to ear. His scalped skull was black with clotted blood.

My ma's body lay between the barn and the cabin, carrion birds picking at her eyes. She lay on her back, her skirts rucked above her hips. Her killer had cut out her sex and removed her left breast, too. Eight Clouds was so disgusted he spat in the dirt. He'd claimed his fair share of trophies, but there was no honor in making a trophy of a woman's breasts or adorning a war spear with the scalp of an young boy. But then, this wasn't the work of Comanches, or Apaches either, for that matter. The horses that left their tracks at the massacre sight had been wearing shoes. This was a White man's crime.

My pa was laying near my ma. He'd been skinned alive, judging by how his limbs were twisted and contorted. As Eight Clouds knelt to examine the butchered remains, he noticed the peeled, snarling muzzle of a wolf jutting from my pa's face.

If Eight Clouds had ever needed proof that the Whites were bad-crazy, this was certainly it. While he had never seen one, himself, Eight Clouds knew the Comanche legends that told how Coyote—the first and greatest of the skinwalkers—had helped the human beings by giving them fire, teaching them language, and interceding with the Great Spirit on their behalf. And damned if the Whites hadn't gone and skinned one alive!

As Eight Clouds stood pondering the immensity of the Whites' folly, he heard what sounded like a baby crying. He looked around and noticed a smokehouse next to the barn, and it was there the crying seemed to be coming from. Like I said, Eight Clouds was inquisitive by nature, so he decided to take a look inside.

My folk's smokehouse wasn't any different from any other smokehouse you'd find at that time—except that there were a couple of human carcasses hanging up with the dressed-out antelopes and jack rabbits. There were also a couple of barrels set behind the door, and it was in one of these that Eight Clouds found a baby wrapped in a blanket, crying to beat the band. That squalling infant was none other than me.

According to Eight Clouds, when he picked me up I instantly stopped crying—a good luck sign according to Comanches—and looked him straight in the eye and smiled. He could tell by the color of my eyes—yellow—that I weren't no human baby. Eight Clouds couldn't believe his luck! Here he'd been worrying about his squaw, Thunder Buffalo Woman, being so sad on account of their son's death, and now he finds a baby skinwalker!

Eight Clouds wasted no time in making a papoose cradle out of some antelope hide and a couple of barrel staves. Pretty soon I accompanied him on his way back to camp, dangling off the horn of the saddle he'd taken off a Mexican *ranchero* he'd killed the season before.

When Eight Clouds got home he showed me to Thunder Buffalo Woman. The prospect of having a young'un around the *tipi* cheered her up to no end. She suggested to Eight Clouds that they take their new son to old Medicine Dog, the tribe's shaman, so I could get myself properly named.

Medicine Dog was a wise man and was quite old, even when I was coming up. He was the one that tended to the tribe when folks fell ill, the one who could look at buffalo afterbirth and tell whether the next season was going to be cold or not, the one who could see the future in the tossing of the bones. He was also in charge of naming the babies born to the tribe—at least the boys.

Medicine Dog was sitting outside his *tipi*, smoking his pipe, looking like he'd been expecting Eight Clouds and Thunder Buffalo Woman the whole time.

"Good day, Medicine Dog."

"Yes, it is a good day, Eight Clouds. What is that Thunder Buffalo Woman is carrying? Have you a new son?"

"I found this child in what was left of a White homestead. I would make him my son." Eight Clouds motioned for Thunder Buffalo Woman to show me to Medicine Dog.

Medicine Dog squinted at me with his left eye—he'd lost the right to an Apache arrowhead years before—and puffed on his pipe. "Your new son is a skinwalker, Eight Clouds. You have brought good luck to the *Penetaka*." Getting to his feet, he motioned for Thunder Buffalo Woman to hand me over. He stood there for a long moment, staring down at me as I played with his medicine necklace, then entered his *tipi*.

Several long minutes passed before he returned, handing me back to my new mother. He nodded to himself, as if pleased by what had transpired. "I offered smoke to the sky and earth and to the four corners of the world and to the Great Spirit. In the smoke I saw the name of your son. It is Little Wolf."

And so that's how I got my first name and became an official member of the Comanche.

When I was younger, folks used to always ask me all kinds of questions: What was it like being raised by injuns? Were the Comanches really murdering red devils? Were they really cannibals?

Well, the Comanche was a warrior society, no two ways about it. They were born horsemen, and proud of their skill in combat. They thought farming and settling down was for weak and cowardly types. They valued bravery and courage above all else, even to the point where a warrior preferred to die young in battle than to grow too old to wage war. Needless to say, they were always fighting someone or another.

Before the Whites came, the Comanche had running feuds with the Pawnee, Cheyenne, Arapaho, Dakota, Kiowa, Apache, Osages, and the

Tonkawas. Later, when the Europeans started trying to settle Texas, they switched over to fighting first the Spanish, then the Anglos full-time. But just so you won't think they were completely inhospitable, they were on decent terms with the Wichitas, Wacos, Tawakonies, and the Kichaies. Most of the time.

As for them being murdering devils—I'll grant you they could be down-right merciless to those they decided were enemies. I've seen Comanche braves bury Apache warriors up to their ears in hot sand and coat their heads with honey so the ants would pick their skulls clean while they were still alive. Then again, I've known a Comanche brave to give water to a White he found dying of gangrene on the open prairie, wrap him in a blanket and sit up with him just so he wouldn't die on his lonesome out in the middle of nowhere. The Comanche could be funny that way.

Like I said, they were a proud people. And fearless. They were the lords of the southern plains and they damn well knew it! The Mexican *rancheros* who first settled the area lived in fear of them. Comanche braves were often in the habit of riding into San Antonio, thronging the streets and public squares, swaggering around like they owned the place. Hell, they even made the townspeople hold the reins of their ponies as they went about raiding the shops and houses! Leastwise, that's what Medicine Dog told me. By the time I was coming up, things were already changing for the Comanche in Texas, and not for the better.

And as for them being cannibals—well, that story got started on account of this band of Comanche called the *Tamina*, also known as the Liver-Eaters. There weren't very many of them and they felt inferior to the bigger, more powerful tribes like the Wasp Riders and the Antelope People. So they came up with this story about eating the livers of their enemies. Now, the Comanche have this big taboo concerning cannibalism, and no Comanche in his right mind would even think about eating another human being, but it sure did make them sound fierce, didn't it?

Unfortunately, most settlers tended to take things at face value and believed they really *were* cannibals. Needless to say, the *Tamina* got exterminated mighty quick.

Thanks to Eight Clouds Rising and Thunder Buffalo Woman, I grew up a happy, healthy child. And, personally, I couldn't have asked for a better childhood. The Comanche cherished their children, seeing how they tended not to produce that many in the first place, and a baby's chance of getting to be a full-grown adult was pretty dicey.

Now one thing you've got to remember about the Comanche; they were a pragmatic people. While they believed in the Great Spirit and the Spirit World beyond this one, they didn't spend much of their spare time fretting over it, unlike other folks, both red and white. They didn't hold to coaxing children toward good behavior by promising them all kinds of sweets after they die, or frighten them away from evil by threatening them with eternal damnation. Instead, the children were shown by word and example that the respect of their fellow tribesmen was to be desired for itself, and the condemnation and contempt of the tribe was to be dreaded and avoided like the plague. Men who were brave and generous were applauded and respected as role models. And since it was practically impossible to live a secluded life in a Comanche encampment, everyone was aware of the conduct of everyone else. It was a remarkably effective way of keeping kids in line, let me tell you.

I learned to ride as soon as I could walk. The Comanche didn't cut you any slack in that area. If you weren't handy with a horse, then what damn good were you? Every Comanche child, boy and girl alike, was expected to know how to handle a full-grown horse all on their own by the age of five. When I was three years old, Eight Clouds lashed me to one of his ponies with a rawhide lariat while he held the pony by a tether, and circled that pony around and around until I literally *became* a part of that animal.

I had plenty of friends, as a child. It didn't make a difference to them that I was White—even less that I was marked as Medicine Dog's understudy as the tribe's shaman. Kids is kids. Like I said, I had plenty of playmates, but my favorites were Small Bear, Flood Moon, Lean Fox, and Quanah, who would later become better known in the world outside the *Comancheria* as Quanah Parker. Quanah and I also had something in common, since he was half-white, the son of a captive woman and the great war-chief, Peta Nocona.

Many a summer day was spent running around the plains, naked as jaybirds, whooping it up in grand old style, playing games like "Grizzly Bear" and hunting hummingbirds and bull-bats with our toy bows and arrows. Sometimes we'd play "camp", and each of the boys would team up with a girl, so they could pretend to be man and wife. The girls would set up windbreaks on the banks of a stream, while us "men" would go out and hunt squirrels, so they could have something to cook for us when we came back to camp. I always made it a point to snag Flood Moon as my "wife" every time.

Sometimes we'd get into mischief—like the time Quanah, Small Bear and I got one of Eight Clouds' ponies and backed into the *tipi* where the elders of the tribe who were too old to wage war spent their time smoking the pipe and chewing the fat about the good old days. Lord, did that thing buck! The old men came pouring out of the smoke lodge like angry bees, shouting and carrying on. Quanah got away, but the old men latched on to me and Small Bear and started making noises about punishing us for our lack of respect. Just then, old Medicine Dog came up and motioned for the elders to be quiet.

"Now, you old fellows, you were once boys like Little Wolf and Small Bear! Don't you remember what devils you were? Forgive them their actions—for will boys not be boys?"

The old men looked at one another and became to laugh and let the matter drop. After all, they were old men—peaceable after all the years spent on the warpath, and not young warriors jealous of their dignity. All in all, they were fine old gents.

Every year, near winter, the various bands of Comanche would gather together. It was a time when news was swapped, friends and family saw one another, marriages and liaisons between different bands became formalized, and the braves took a breather from the hunting and raiding that filled the rest of their year.

There were several different branches of Comanche back then, some of which were more powerful than others. Like I said before, I was a member of the *Penateka*, or the Wasp Band. Others included the *Yamparika* (the Yap-Eaters), the *Kweharena* (the Antelope People), the *Kutsuaka* (the Buffalo-Eaters), the *Pahuraix* (the Water Horses), and the *Wa'ai* (the Wormy Penis), to name just a few. But even collected together in all their glory, there couldn't have been more than ten thousand Comanche, total. So you can imagine the damage that was done when smallpox broke out in 1850. I couldn't have been more than six or seven at the time, but I remember it being worse than any nightmare I'd ever had—or ever will again.

It was then that my adopted mother, Thunder Buffalo Woman, died. It broke poor Eight Clouds' heart, and he was never quite the same after that, even though he ended up taking her younger sister, Little Dove, to wife a year or two later.

I was twelve years old by the time I finally got to go on my first real buffalo hunt. I was riding with Eight Clouds and several other braves from our band, including one that went by the name Grass Rope. Grass Rope's specialty was laying low in the grass and sneaking up on the buffalo while they were grazing. He wore a coyote skin draped over his shoulders to mask his scent. Since coyotes were always haunting the fringes of the herds, looking to scavenge afterbirth during the calving season, the buffalo didn't pay much mind, since they were too small to bring down even the youngest calf.

When we spied the herd, Grass Rope got off his pony and motioned for me to follow him. Holding his bow at the ready, he got down on his hands and knees and started creeping through the prairie grass in the direction of the herd. I followed him, doing my best to keep myself upwind of the grazing buffalo. I was very proud that a skilled stalker such as Grass Rope had chosen me to accompany him, and I was determined to cover myself with glory the best I could. However, as we crept closer and closer to the herd, something strange began to happen.

My sense of smell had always been acute, but for some reason it was incredibly keen that particular day. I could smell the grass as the sun dried the dew from its stems, the pungent odor of buffalo wool, the reek of their flops—but, more importantly, I could smell the coyote pelt Grass Rope was wearing. I caught its scent and for the briefest moment I <u>knew</u> everything there was to know about the beast it had once belonged to: its sex, age, health, and social standing in its pack. The surge of recognition was so powerful, I had to lower my head and whine.

Grass Rope gave me a hard look. Hunting was serious business and it was no time for foolish pranks. "Be quiet, Little Wolf!" he whispered.

I tried to keep silent, but I was suddenly gripped by a strange fire that burned deep inside me like a banked coal. I bit my tongue to keep from crying out, causing blood to flow. The fire in my belly was growing and my skin felt as if it was covered with biting ants. My bones seemed to be inflating inside my flesh, and for a fleeting second I was afraid I'd been bitten by a rattlesnake without knowing it and was dying.

Grass Rope grew very angry with my whimpering and twitching and turned to give me the sharp side of his tongue, but what he saw made him forget about scolding me. Even though I was in great pain, I knew something must be very wrong, because his face suddenly went pale under his paint. Then the next thing I know, the buffalo start to bellow and stampede, running away from us.

Without thinking, I leapt to my feet and started chasing after the fleeing buffalo, running like a band of Apache were at my heels. I vaguely remember seeing some of the other braves from the hunting party sitting astride their ponies, pointing in my direction open-mouthed, their lances and arrows forgotten. Then I spotted a young buffalo calf that had lost its mother and, panicking, placed itself on the fringes of the herd. I closed the distance between us, separating it from its fellows, snapping at its trembling flanks. The frightened youngster bellowed for its mother, but it was too late. She was already miles away, trapped within the nucleus of the herd, helpless to defend her errant child.

Without realizing what I was doing, I leapt onto the calf's wooly back, sinking my talons and teeth into its neck. The calf shrieked and, overbalanced, fell on top of me. (And seventy-plus pounds of buffalo calf is nothing to sneeze at, believe me.) Although I had the wind knocked out of me, I refused to let go. The dying calf jerked and kicked, but to no avail, as I tore out its throat with my bare teeth.

I stared down at the calf as it bled its life onto the prairie grass and threw back my head and howled in triumph. And it was only then, as I licked the fresh blood off my snout, that I realized I was covered in fur and that my hands boasted cruel, curved talons in place of fingernails.

Eight Clouds rode up, reigning his pony at a safe distance. The pony rolls its eyes and stamped the ground nervously, uncertain whether to stay or flee. Eight Clouds looked the same way.

"My son—are you still inside?"

"Yes, father. I am still here." My voice was strangely distorted and gravelly, like an animal given the power of human speech.

Eight Clouds nodded, relieved. "You have hunted well. You bring honor to our lodge."

Grass Rope rode up, looking positively thunderstruck. "What manner of thing is this?" he demanded, pointing at me.

Eight Clouds smiled, proud enough to bust. "It is not a thing, it is my son, Little Wolf."

Grass Rope shook his head in amazement. "He is a walking wolf!

Never have I seen such a thing!"

And that's how I got my adult name—and how I shapeshifted for the first time in my life. I didn't realize it then, but my boyhood days were gone forever and things were soon going to change in ways I had no way of foreseeing.

CHAPTER TWO

After my first experience with shapeshifting, my life amongst the tribe became very different. The first, and most radical, change came with my apprenticeship to Medicine Dog. The old shaman had always taken a grandfatherly interest in me, but now I was expected to move my meager belongings from my father's *tipi* into his.

Medicine Dog was a wise man, full of knowledge acquired during a long and eventful life. I remember I once asked him if he hated the Apache for blinding him in the right eye, and he laughed.

"My life was good in the old days. But it was the life of a fool. I was a mighty warrior back then. I was very proud. Too proud. I was vain and my vanity made me weak. When the Apache took away my eye, I may have lost the ability to see things in this world, but I gained the ability to see into the Spirit World. Should I hate the Apache for giving me such a wonderful gift, Walking Wolf?"

Like I said, Medicine Dog was a wise man, but I was young and still aching to prove myself as a brave, like other boys, so I tended to ignore a lot of what he told me. I genuinely liked the old fellow, but it chafed me that I had to tend his fire and fetch his water, just like a woman, while my old playmates Quanah and Small Bear were off hunting buffalo or out on pony raids. It pains me to look back and realize just how big a fool I was back then. But Medicine Dog didn't seem to mind it—I guess he expected a certain amount of thick-headedness on my part.

Still, I did learn things, in spite of myself. Medicine Dog schooled me as to the prayers necessary to ensure successful raids and hunts, the prayers that correctly guide the dead to the Spirit World, and the prayers that confuse evil spirits so they can't tell which *tipi* is the one they're looking for at night. He also taught me breathing and meditation exercises that helped me control my shapeshifting, so I could summon what he called my "true" skin at will and with minimum discomfort. He also warned me to never tell a White that I was a skinwalker.

"Whites are jealous of things they don't understand. Of things they can not have or do. That is why the human beings—we who lived on this land before they came—have had so much trouble with them. If you tell a White that you have more than one skin—they will try and take it away from you. Just like they did your natural father. Be very careful who you show your true-skin to, Walking Wolf, if you want to keep it on your bones."

Medicine Dog also told me stories of Coyote, the trickster god from whom all skinwalkers are descended. I reckon it was on account of their most popular folk hero having the head of a coyote that the Plains Indians I knew back then rarely got upset by me sprouting hair, claws, and fangs. Instead of seeing a monster, they saw a god. After all, according to their folklore, Coyote was responsible in part for human beings coming into existence in the first place, and he gave them fire and corn and the buffalo to make their life on earth an easier one. While theirs was a far more reasonable reaction to my condition, it did nothing to prepare me for what I would run up against in the white man's world, although I did get a taste of rejection early on.

I've already mentioned Flood Moon. As I'd said earlier, I'd known her all my life. She was a pretty thing, by Comanche standards, with long, straight black hair woven into two thick braids, and she had this shy way of smiling that was enough to melt my heart every time she looked at me.

I'd known from the time I was seven years old that Flood Moon was going to be mine, and once, when we were still very young, I even got her to promise to be my wife when we grew up. But that was back when I was Little Wolf. Things became very different once I became Walking Wolf and, like the young fool I was, I refused to admit it.

As I said, most of the Comanche took my being not exactly human as a matter of course. Occasionally I'd get asked by an exasperated older sister to threaten to eat a misbehaving youngster, but that was quite rare, and the children usually knew better. Flood Moon, however, was one of the few who had genuine trouble with my condition.

Before I'd learned how to shift she'd been all smiles and flirts, but when we came riding back from the hunt that day—me still wearing my true-skin—she grew ashen-faced and hurried into her family's *tipi* and wouldn't come out.

Despite Flood Moon's sudden coolness towards me, I was still sweet on her. Whenever I could manage it, I would sneak away from Medicine Dog's *tipi* and loiter near the creek and wait for her to pass by on her way to gather firewood or water.

One thing you've got to understand about the Comanche way of courting is that it was all very proper. Boys and girls, after a certain age, weren't allowed to be in one another's company unchaperoned. And there's nothing more bashful than a lovestruck brave. So young lovers had to sneak what time they could together during daylight.

I spent agonizing hours waiting for just a glimpse of Flood Moon. And when I finally did get a few minutes alone with her, I was so tongue-tied I never said much. She would tolerate my presence well enough if I was wearing my human skin, but if I was wearing my true-skin she'd be as nervous as a pony staked out to trap a mountain cat, hurrying through her chores as fast as she could, often slopping half the water she'd drawn from the creek on her way back to camp.

Although I was nowhere near as bold as some of my friends, who would lie outside their chosen one's *tipís* at night and whisper promises of love and marriage through the seams in the tent-skins, I was determined to make Flood Moon mine, and set about saving up ponies to give her family as marriage tribute. But first I had to make sure her father and brothers would not turn down my offer.

I talked one of the older, more respected women in the tribe into approaching Flood Moon's father, Calling Owl, and putting my case to him. Calling Owl was very pleased that his daughter had caught the fancy of the tribe's resident skinwalker, as it meant good luck for his family. But when Flood Moon heard that I'd sent the old woman over, she begged her father to ask for thirty horses. Although Calling Owl saw having a skinwalker as a son-in-law a good thing, he loved his daughter enough to agree to her wishes—at least for the moment.

When the old woman told me how much Calling Owl wanted for Flood Moon, I was dismayed. Thirty ponies! I was thirteen years old and only had one pony to my name—and that was one Eight Clouds had given me! How was I to get thirty ponies? Well, the same way any Comanche got ponies—it was up to me to steal some.

Now, let me digress a bit and explain horse-stealing, Comanche-style. The Comanche set a great deal of stock in horseflesh—and if there was ever a people born to ride, it was them. Compared to, say, the Cheyenne, the Comanche were a short, squat race. On the ground, they were far from graceful—but on the back of a horse, they were poetry in motion. Since their society revolved around the horse, the Comanche used them as a rate of exchange. And the mark of a rich man was to have more ponies than he could ever possibly ride. A truly powerful chief would have dozens, if not hundreds, of ponies, most of them taken in raids from either other tribes or settlers. And while Whites considered horse-stealing the lowest thing next to snatching an infant nursing at its mothers' breast and dashing its brains out against a wall—if not lower—Indians saw it as a truly worthwhile skill. In fact, when they weren't out hunting buffalo, the Plains tribes seemed to spend the vast majority of their spare time stealing horses from one another. Still, it wasn't without its hazards.

Although I was apprenticed to Medicine Dog, he did not forbid me riding with the others on raids. After all, how else was I going to make myself a respected member of the band if I didn't distinguish myself on the warpath? Medicine Dog might have had one eye in the Spirit World, but he was a practical man. So I began joining the raiding parties, doing my best to help steal as many ponies as possible, so I could benefit when the spoils were divided at the end of a successful raid. Still, it was slow going for a brave as young as myself, since the elder warriors got preferential treatment.

A year passed and all I had to show for it were ten horses. I still ached for Flood Moon, and the waiting was driving me to distraction. Medicine Dog cautioned me and suggested I had much to learn about patience. Many Comanche braves waited until they were well into their twenties and were solidly established with many ponies and buffalo robes to their name, before taking a wife. But my blood burned and I was convinced that the only way I was ever to know happiness was if I took Flood Moon into my *tipi* as my wife.

One night the Apaches raided our herd when most of the braves were away hunting, and all of my ponies were stolen. At first I was devastated. It had taken me so long to acquire those ten ponies, only to have them stolen! Then my grief turned to anger and I became determined to go after the Apaches and reclaim my horses, plus as many more as I possibly could!

I set off after the Apache raiders on Medicine Dog's pony that very night, armed with nothing but a bow, some arrows, and a knife. They had stolen close to a hundred horses and their trail was not hard to find. Still, they had a head start, and I knew once they made it to the hill country I wouldn't stand a chance.

I caught up with the raiders near dawn, several miles west of the camp. They had decided that they had gotten away scot free and had slackened their pace enough to stop and have a brief meal along the banks of a dry riverbed. As I watched them from a distance, I could tell the six braves responsible for the raid were very young—some no older than myself—and overconfident. A couple of them had rifles, which added to their cockiness. It occurred to me that my decision to leave ahead of my fellow braves had been foolhardy. Here I was alone, armed with nothing but a bow and a knife, while my enemies carried guns. There was no way I could reclaim the horses without exposing myself to attack... Unless I took a lesson from the trickster himself.

The Apache brave keeping watch was genuinely surprised to see me. Then again, he probably hadn't seen many upright wolves dressed in breechclouts and buckskin leggins before.

"Greetings, Brother Human Being," I smiled, licking my snout and speaking passable Apache. "I am Coyote."

The Apache was so thunderstruck his knees began to wobble like a newborn colt's. He called out to his fellow braves, who hurried to see what was the matter. Naturally, they were equally amazed to see the trickster-god of legend standing before them.

"I hope I am not bothering you fine warriors this beautiful morning," I said, gesturing to the rising sun. "But I was passing by on my way to visit the Great Spirit, to ask him certain favors for those who are my friends, and could not help but notice what a beautiful herd of horses you have."

"Th-thank you, Father Coyote," stammered the raiding party's leader. "You are going to see the Great Spirit?"

"Yes! Those blessed to Coyote receive good hunting and many coup against their enemies. Did I mention before how fine your horses are?"

The Apache braves looked amongst themselves then glanced back at the herd.

"Yes, the Great Spirit shows great respect for those who prove their generosity to others," I continued, lying through my fangs. "Why, just the other day, the Wasp Band of the Comanche gave me ten horses..."

"Ten! Is that all?" snorted the Apache leader. "I would not call that generous!"

"Perhaps so," I said. "But in any case, I must be on my way...Have a good journey, friend human beings."

As I made to leave, the lead Apache called after me. "Father Coyote! We can not let you leave without giving you a gift!"

"A gift, you say? What of?"

"Ponies."

"How many?"

I could tell he was trying to figure out how many ponies would be enough—he surely didn't want to offend a god important enough to put his case to the Great Spirit.

"Twenty—?"

I had him dangling but good. "Twenty? What a coincidence! Why, the Kiowa gave me a string of twenty ponies just last week..."

"Forty then!" The Apache blurted.

I made a great show of scratching my chin in deliberation. I was actually enjoying the part of sly trickster, but I knew I was running the risk of irate braves unwilling to part with their share of the night's raid calling my bluff.

"Forty? Friend human being, you are truly a generous and great man! I shall be certain to mention your name first when I speak with the Great Spirit!"

You can imagine how surprised my tribe was when I came riding back into camp, leading a string of forty ponies. When I told Medicine Dog how I succeeding in tricking the Apaches into returning my original ten horses, plus thirty more, the old coot came close to busting a gut laughing.

"Walking Wolf, you are indeed touched by the hand of Coyote! Only he could have wrested forty ponies from Apache braves without resorting to violence!"

I showed up the next afternoon in front of Calling Owl's *tipi* with the thirty horses needed to buy his daughter from him. Calling Owl was very pleased. Flood Moon, on the other hand, looked less than thrilled. She stood there, staring at her feet, as her father talked about how he was looking forward to grandchildren. After Calling Owl and I had sealed the transaction with a smoke from his pipe, Flood Moon went into her family's *tipi* for the last time and removed her sleeping roll, her feeding bowl, and a few other belongings and, walking behind me with her head still bowed, followed me to my *tipi*. Suddenly I was married. Like I said, the Comanche were practical people who didn't go in much for ceremony.

"How do you like your new home, Flood Moon? Isn't this better than the lean-to I built when we were children and played camp together?"

Flood Moon grunted and started to unroll her sleeping blankets. She didn't seem too impressed by her new home, but I tried not to let her lack of enthusiasm bother me. I reached out to embrace her, only to have her go rigid in my arms.

"Flood Moon, what is the matter?" I lifted her chin with my thumb and forefinger, but she looked away.

"I am frightened, Walking Wolf. I have never been with a man before."

"But I am your husband! You need not fear me!"

She looked at me from the corner of her eyes, smiling shyly. "Go outside and smoke your pipe. When you finish, I will be waiting for you inside my sleeping robes, ready to be your wife."

I was ready for her to be my wife right *then*, but I knew better than to hurry her. Comanche women could be powerful shy, but once you got them under the sleeping robes they were randier than a she-bear in heat. So I went outside, had me a smoke and watched the sun go down.

When I'd finished my pipe I got up and stood by the tent flap and called softly to my wife. "Flood Moon? Are you ready? I'm coming in now..."

The moment I set foot in the *tipi*, something crashed into the back of my head, knocking me to the ground, where I stayed—unconscious—until the next morning. When I came to, I discovered Flood Moon and her belongings were gone. The only thing she'd left behind was the grinding stone she'd used to coldcock me. Judging from the amount of blood on the grinding stone, it looked like she'd been meaning to crack my braincase open for the whole world to see what a witless fool I was.

I staggered out of my *tipi* to find Medicine Dog waiting on me, puffing on his pipe. "So. You aren't dead," he said, by way of greeting.

"Where's Flood Moon? Where is my wife?"

"She is gone."

"Gone? Where did she go?"

Medicine Dog shrugged. "I do not know. She and Small Bear were very scared. They thought they had killed you."

"Small Bear? Flood Moon is with Small Bear?" I could feel the anger swell inside me. My head still ached and I did not want to hear what Medicine Dog was telling me.

"Yes. They left together last night."

My best friend. The woman I loved. Both had betrayed me. And worse, they had robbed me of my pride. I had been made to look a fool in the eyes of the tribe. Such a crime against my honor could not go unpunished. My distress was quite obvious and Medicine Dog put aside his pipe and tried to calm me.

"My son, do not let your anger drive you to do something worse than foolish."

My head throbbed like a war drum and I doubled over, pushing at the sides of my skull to keep them from exploding outward. My anger was fueling the pain inside my head, forcing my body into its true-form. Medicine Dog stepped away from me. I had the blood-lust on me and he knew words would be useless. Snarling like a beast, I fled the camp. I had the scent of Flood Moon and Small Bear and I was determined to hunt them down and make them pay for their treachery.

It did not take me long to catch up with them. Like most *vargr*, I am a tireless runner and the rage burning deep inside me kept me from growing weary. Although they had a whole night and day's head start on horseback, I found them not long after dark.

I saw their fire long before I saw them. They were alone except for each other and their horses, huddled against the coming night. Careful to keep upwind of their mounts, least they catch my scent and alarm Small Bear, I circled their camp, listening to them as they talked.

I could tell from their words and actions that they had been lovers for some time. Small Bear sat with his rifle at the ready, Flood Moon pressed close to him. The sight of my best friend sharing an intimacy with my wife that I myself had never known stoked my anger even higher, until everything I saw was covered by a blood-red scrim.

One of the ponies wickered nervously and Small Bear tightened his grip on his gun, peering anxiously into the dark beyond the fire as he got to his feet.

Flood Moon looked up at her lover, knuckling the sleep from her eyes. "Small Bear—what is wrong?"

"There is something out there."

I came in low, tackling him from behind, snarling like a rabid wolf. Small Bear's rifle discharged as he hit the ground. Flood Moon screamed out her lover's name, driving the knife she'd kept hidden in her blanket into my right side. I yowled in pain and made to grab at the intruding blade, giving Small Bear the chance to roll free and get back on his feet. Unsheathing his own knife, he made to drive it into my heart. Growling, I knocked the weapon from his hands and pounced on him as a coyote would a prairie dog, my teeth sinking deep into his soft, hairless throat.

I don't want people reading this to think the fight was one-sided. Small Bear was a strong, swift brave, and he did not surrender easily to death. Still, I tore at his struggling body with my talons, gleefully ripping his bowels free of his stomach. Small Bear's liver, glistening brown-red in the campfire, lay on the prairie grass, and without pausing to think, I snapped the tender morsel up and devoured it on the spot.

Wiping my muzzle on my forearm, I turned my yellow gaze to Flood Moon, who stood transfixed, staring in horror at the ruined remains of her lover. Smiling, I plucked her knife from my side as if it was no more bothersome to me than a thorn.

"Wife," I said, holding up the dripping blade. "Is this how you greet your husband?"

She gave a sob of fear and turned to flee, but I was too fast for her. I grabbed her by her braids, wrapping them around my forepaws so her face would be within biting distance. Her eyes were huge with fear and the smell of her terror radiated from her like heat from the sun. Grinning, I licked her face with my tongue, laughing when she shuddered and began to cry.

I took her there, beside the cooling body of her lover. She screamed and whimpered and pleaded with me repeatedly as I raped her—for that was what I did, I don't deny it—but all it did was increase my determination to punish her even farther. By the time my lust had run its course Flood Moon bled from dozens of deep bites and scratches on her breasts, belly, buttocks and thighs. Sated at last, I pulled myself from her quivering, sobbing body and collapsed beside her in a deep slumber.

I awoke to find Flood Moon astride me, ready to plunge the knife she retrieved into my chest. I'll never forget looking up into the face of the woman who, until that day, I had loved with all my life and heart, her face rendered almost unrecognizable by the bruises I'd given her. The hatred that burned in her eyes was so intense, so all-consuming it was like a blow. She screamed in triumph as the knife sank up to the hilt in my chest.

My first reaction was a primal one—without thinking, I swiped at her as she struggled to pull the blade free for a second strike, my talons sinking into the soft flesh of her jugular. Flood Moon clutched her throat, a rattling gasp coming from her lips. I had sliced open her wind-pipe.

Struggling to get to my feet, I tugged at the knife wedged in my ribs. I was fully expecting to die, but to my surprise, after an initial spurt of blood, my wound sealed itself. The same could not be said for Flood Moon, who lay writhing on the ground at my feet, blood spurting between her fingers.

I felt as if I had woken from a bad dream only to find myself trapped within a nightmare. My head no longer ached and I was empty of the anger that had driven me so relentlessly to such a horrible end. I looked around me as if in a daze. When I saw the mutilated body of Small Bear, I cried out in horror. Even as I closed my eyes to the murder I had committed, my memory replayed for me how I had brutally violated the only woman I had ever loved. When I opened them again, it was to see that Flood Moon, in her last moments, had crawled next to Small Bear to die.

I buried them there, side by side, on the lone prairie. I wept as I dug their common grave with the knife Flood Moon had planted in my heart, mourning as much for myself as for my victims, for I knew I could not return to my tribe after what I had done.

I grew physically ill at the thought of how Eight Clouds Rising, Medicine Dog, Quanah, Peta Nocona and the others would react once they learned of my crimes. Flood Moon and Small Bear had wounded my pride, but the punishment I had meted out to them was beyond all decent measure. And, to make matters worse, I had compounded my sin by breaking the Comanche taboo against cannibalism.

I was ashamed and frightened by what I had done. I had lost control of my baser nature and allowed it to revel in the pain of others. I felt sick to my soul. I decided I needed to know more about my strange powers and the beast inside me, lest I lose control again and harm someone else dear to me. There was only one way I could learn more about myself. I decided it was finally time for me to go into the White Man's world.

CHAPTER THREE

My decision to abandon the way of the Comanche for the White Man's society was not an easy one. Even though, technically, I was one of their number, I had no reason to love or trust Whites.

First of all, it was Whites who killed my natural family. I'd known that before I learned to walk, since Eight Clouds made a point of telling me, early on, the story of how I came to be his son. Secondly, throughout my years as a member of the Wasp Riders, I had ample occasion to see how treacherous Whites could be. They had broken numerous treaties and waged war against the Comanche in a cowardly fashion for years. And third, it was the Whites who were responsible for the epidemics of cholera, diphtheria, influenza, measles, smallpox, and syphilis that spread through the tribe like brushfire, claiming brave, elder, squaw, and papoose alike.

The Whites seemed stricken with a craziness the Comanche—and all other Indians—were at a loss to comprehend. Their buffalo hunters killed more than they could possibly eat in a lifetime. Their farmers wrapped the land in barbed wire and claimed the dirt below and the sky above their property. Still, for madmen, they were privy to immense power. The iron horses and the buffalo-guns that could kill from a mile away

31

were truly impressive. So, was it not possible they might have knowledge as to how I might better control my wolf-self?

I knew better than to ride up to the nearest settlement and expect to be welcomed with open arms. What with my long dark hair and sun-browned skin, I looked more Indian than White. I was likely to catch a bullet between the eyes before I had a chance to dismount. Besides, my English was pretty bad—in fact, non-existent. No, if I was going to introduce myself to White society, it was going to have to be through an intermediary of some kind.

A week or more after I had voluntarily banished myself, I came upon a black man traveling alone across the prairie, driving a wagon pulled by oxen. When he saw my pony approaching, he reigned his oxen to a halt and pulled out a rifle and rested it across his knees, watching me cautiously.

As I drew nearer I recognized him as the man called Buffalo Face, who traded on occasion with the Wasp Riders, swapping rifles, ammunition and liquor for ponies.

"Good day, Buffalo-Face," I said, speaking in the mixture of Spanish and Comanche dialect that was reserved for dealing with traders.

He squinted at me and spat a stream of tobacco juice out of the side of his mouth. He was a big, powerfully built man with skin that gleamed like polished stone and a mass of dark, nappy wool that hung to his shoulders, which was the reason the Comanche had given him his name.

"You Comanche, ain't ya?"

"I am Walking Wolf of the *Penateka*."

Buffalo-Face's shoulders relaxed. "Walking Wolf? You're Eight Clouds' boy, am I right? What you doin' way the hell out here, son? You out scoutin' buffalo?"

"I'm looking for Whites."

"Why? You on the warpath?"

"No. I want to go into the White Man's world and learn how it works."

Buffalo-Face spat another streamer of tobacco juice, narrowly missing the rump of his lead ox. "Why the hell would you want to do something like that?"

"Because I am White, too."

Buffalo-Face squinted harder, leaning forward a bit. "Damned if it ain't so! You *are* white under all that dirt and paint! Imagine that."

"Will you take me to the Whites, Buffalo-Face?"

Buffalo-Face frowned and rubbed his chin for a spell, occasionally giving me a look from under his knitted brow. After a long minute he shrugged. "Son, you're a fool to ask me, and I'm an even bigger fool for sayin' yes. Hitch your pony to the back of the cart there and ride up front with me. I could stand the company. It gets pretty lonesome out here with no one but Goodness and Mercy here to talk to," he said, gesturing to the yoked oxen.

Although the idea of riding on anything besides a pony was alien to me, I did as he asked and joined him on the wagon seat. The oxen did not move nearly as quickly as horses, but they plodded along without protest or halting.

During the course of our first day together, Buffalo-Face told me things about himself. I learned that he had been born a slave in some place called Alabama, that his mother had been raped at the age of twelve by the white overseer of the plantation she served on, and that he had killed a man—the same overseer who'd fathered him—in order to escape when he was sixteen. I also learned that he had left behind a wife and two, possibly three, children, in a place called Philadelphia.

Buffalo-Face shook his head and spat a streamer of tobacco juice, drowning a blue-bottle fly perched on Goodness' left rump. "I'll be damned if I can figger out why you want to get yourself turned white. Sure, they're your own kind, but you're as much a stranger to their ways as any full-blooded injun. Hell, I spent the first sixteen years of my life doin' my best to put distance `tween me and white folk. I thought once I was free, things would be different for me.

"Well, things may have been better for me, up north, but they weren't no different. I was still a nigger, far as anyone was concerned. I could never get my wife to understand that bein' free of the plantation weren't enough for me. I didn't escape Alabama so's I could turn myself into a white nigger and spend the rest of my life tryin' to be like them.

"Six years ago I come out west. I'm still a nigger, far as the folks out here are concerned. But at least I can at least spit without hittin' one of `em," he demonstrated. "I can be my own boss and do as I please. If white folks could look inside my head and see how much I hated `em, I'd be hanging from the nearest cottonwood faster'n a jackrabbit. So instead of shootin' whites and burnin' their homes to the ground, I get my satisfaction by peddlin' guns to the Comanches. Way I sees it, they got as much reason as me to be fond of the whites."

That night we set up camp and Buffalo-Face served up black beans, dry bread, and hot coffee. I'd never had coffee before, and I promptly spat it out. Buffalo-Face laughed as I grimaced and wiped my mouth with handfuls of grass.

"Give yourself a week, son, and you'll be suckin' it up like it was mother's milk!"

I liked Buffalo-Face. Outside of a Mexican boy stolen from a *ranchero* during one of our winter encampments, he was the only non-Comanche I had ever spent any time with. I wondered if I ought to tell him that I was a skinwalker, but I remembered Medicine Dog's warning concerning who I showed my true-skin to. Buffalo-Face wasn't a White, but he wasn't an Indian, either. I fell asleep, pondering the question of whether I should tell him more about myself.

When I awoke, the coffee pot was on the fire but Buffalo-Face was nowhere to be seen. I found him down by the creek, stripped to his waist, washing his face and upper body. His muscular back was covered from shoulder to waist by scars that ran from rib to rib. The wounds were very old, some of them five or six deep in places. I watched him for a few more seconds, then returned to the camp.

When Buffalo-Face came back, he had replaced his shirt and was shrugging into his braces. He bent to pour coffee into a dented tin cup. "You sure you want to go ahead with this plan of yours? You seen the stripes on my back when I was washing at the creek. *That's* what white folk had to offer me."

"Medicine Dog told me that Whites are crazy. Is this true?"

Buffalo-Face nodded and swallowed his coffee, grimacing, whether from the bitterness of the brew or his memories was hard to say. "That they are. But not fall-down, foam-at-the-mouth crazy, though. Whites are singular creatures. They ain't part of nothing but themselves, not even other whites. Mebbe that's what makes 'em act so snake-bit.

"Let me give you a bit of free advice, son. Whatever you do, always watch your back. Whites may hate niggers, injuns, kikes and chinks—but that don't mean they love their own kind. If they can find a way to get what they want and leave you bleedin' and nekkid in the snow, they will. Whites ain't out for no one but themselves. Bear that in mind whenever you're dealing with 'em—don't matter if they're a man of the cloth, an old spinster lady, or a young'un in knee-pants. Whatever you do, don't trust 'em any farther than you can throw 'em."

I spent most of the next four weeks learning to speak English—at least talk it good enough to get myself understood. Buffalo-Face was astonished at how quickly I picked up the lingo. I didn't realize it at the time, but I have a natural aptitude for learning languages. At last count, I've become fluent in thirty-seven, including Swahili, Cantonese, Mongolian, and Aborigine.

On the second week on the trail together, we were sitting around one night, drinking hot coffee and studying the stars overhead, when Buffalo-face looks at me and says; "Well, if you're so god-damned set on bein' part of the white man's world, you've got to have you a white man's name. Walkin' Wolf might be a mighty fine name for a Comanche, but it ain't no kind of name for a white man."

Buffalo-Face worked his chaw real thoughtful for a second. "You wouldn't happen to know your real name, would you? No? In that case, we'll have to come up with a name on our own... Wouldn't be the first time a man's named himself out here...

"Let's see now... William's a good name. But you're too young for a serious first name like that. How about Will? Naw... You look more like a Billy to me. Billy. Yeah, that sounds good! But Billy what? Smith or Jones are popular, but not exactly what you'd call distinctive. You want yourself a handle that folks'll remember..." Buffalo-Face's bloodshot eye wandered about our camp, his gaze finally settling on the cook-fire. He grinned suddenly, displaying tobacco-stained teeth. "That's it! Skillet! Billy Skillet! How that sound to you, Walkin' Wol—I mean, Billy?"

I gave it a thought, rolling the name around on my tongue for effect. Billy Skillet. Damned if it didn't feel good in my mouth.

"I like it."

Buffalo-Face let out with a laugh like a wild ass in heat. "Then that's who you are, by damn! Billy Skillet! And don't let no one tell you otherwise!"

So that's now I got my white name. Here I was, barely fifteen years old, and I already had me three—possibly four—names. That's as many, or more, than a Comanche brave gets in a whole lifetime!

I'll always remember that night—how the stars glinted in the sky, how the air smelled of ox dung and coffee grounds, the sound of tobacco-juice sizzling in the campfire. I was enjoying the best of both worlds there—Indian and White—without knowing it. I knew there was no way it was going to last forever, but I had no idea how long it'd be before I would know such peace again.

At the end of four weeks we'd finally come within passing distance of a white settlement big enough to think it was a town. Buffalo-Face took me up on a rise that overlooked the slap-dash collection of wood houses and dirt streets.

"That there's Vermillion, Texas. White folks live there. Few Meskins, too, but mostly whites. You'll excuse me if I don't walk you down to the city limits. I don't do no tradin' with white folk in Texas—except for Spaniards. They're pure out-and-out businessmen, them Spaniards. Don't give a rat's ass what a color a man's skin is, long as his coins are silver or gold. Don't care if you're selling liquor and guns to injuns, either. Man's business is a man's business."

Buffalo-Face turned to look at me, shaking his head sadly. "You've been good company on the trail, boy. I'm sorry to see you go. I just hope you don't turn mean-crazy once you get yourself civilized. I reckon there are kindly white folks out there, somewheres. Lord knows, I never run across one. But, then again, I ain't never seen an elephant, either. Mebbe your luck will be better'n mine on that count. Just remember what I told you, and you'll stand a half-way decent chance dealin' with `em."

I threw my arms around his wide, scarred shoulders and hugged him as I would my own father. "Thank you for giving me my new name, Buffalo-Face."

"Shoot, t'weren't nothing, son," he said smiling. Suddenly his smile disappeared and he wagged a tobacco-stained finger in my face. "But whatever you do, don't tell `em you've been keepin' company with a black man who sells guns to injuns! All that'll do is put you on the wrong foot from the get-go!"

With that he returned to his ox-cart laden with contraband. The last I saw of him, he was spitting tobacco juice and snapping his whip over Goodness and Mercy, cursing a blue-streak. We never met again, although

I heard, years later, that he had run afoul of white settlers in Oklahoma in '61, who—upon learning he sold guns and ammunition to the Comanche and Apache—lynched him from the nearest cottonwood tree.

CHAPTER FOUR

The first thing that struck me about the town of Vermillion, Texas was its smell. To say that it reeked would be kind. Not that living the Indian life made me all pure and natural. Indian camps were hardly known for their sanitary conditions. What with dozens of horses and people living, eating, breathing, and crapping side-by-side, things tended to get mighty ripe. However, the Indians were nomads, and when their surroundings got too fragrant, so to speak, they'd up and find themselves a new campsite. Whites, on the other hand, had a tendency to stay put in their own stink.

Vermillion was no more than a collection of ramshackle one-story clapboard buildings and adobe huts occupied by forty-seven souls—give or take a couple of Mexicans. There was a combination saloon and bawdy house, a feed and seed store, a general store, and a blacksmith who also stood in as the local undertaker. All of these businesses lined a broad unpaved street that, thanks to the rainy season, was composed of equal parts mud and shit, both human and horse. This foul mixture, when churned into the proper consistency by passing traffic, was capable of sucking a boot clean off a man's foot and swallowing it whole, never to be seen again. Because of this, wooden boardwalks fronted both sides of the street, with haphazardly-placed planks connecting the two.

In retrospect, Vermillion was a wretched little one-horse town, cling-
ing to the edge of the Texas frontier like a tick on a dog's ear. But as far as
I was concerned, it might as well have been the mysterious Philadelphia
Buffalo Face had spoken of.

The moment I rode into town, I was aware of all eyes being on me.
Everyone stopped what they were doing to stare after me, watching me
the same way a cougar does a wolf that's wandered into its territory. What
with my pony and my braids and breechcloth, I must have looked like a
full-blooded Comanche brave.

I dismounted in front of the saloon and tied my pony to the hitching
post. The moment I turned around, I found myself looking at a big tin
star. The star was pinned on the chest of a burly, red-faced man with a
drooping yellow mustache and a shock of blonde hair, atop of which rested
a derby hat of fashionable make. A Colt six-shooter jutted from the holster strapped to the big man's hip.

"What you think you're doin' here, injun?" the big man growled,
letting his hand drop onto the butt of his gun.

I smiled as Buffalo-Face had instructed me, averting my eyes and
bobbing my head in ritual subservience. "My name is Billy Skillet. I have
come here to be White."

The big man's brows knitted together and his eyes lost their hard-
ness. "Come again?"

"I am White like you," I hurried to explain. "I was taken by
Comanches when very young, but now I have come to my people to learn
to be White."

He pushed back his derby and scratched his head, looking me up
and down. "Well, I'll be dipped in shit and shot for stinkin'! You *are*
white, ain't you!"

"Perhaps I can be of some assistance, Marshal..?"

My mouth went dry in terror at the sight of the tall, broad-shouldered man striding towards me. In place of eyes, he had two black circles, like the empty sockets of a skull.

"He has no eyes!" I cried out, pointing at the fearsome apparition bearing down on us.

The eyeless man laughed at my show of alarm and lifted the smoked glass spectacles he wore to allow me a glimpse of the eyes underneath.

"You needn't fear me, my son—I have two eyes, just as God intended."

The Marshal scowled at the eyeless man. "Oh, it's you, Near."

"*Reverend* Near," the older man corrected, adjusting the lapels of his dusty frock coat.

"What have you," grunted the Marshal. "What do you want, *Reverend*?"

"I couldn't help but overhear this poor lad's tale of woe," exclaimed Reverend Near, flashing me a sympathetic smile. "Back in Chicago, I read stories of how the heathen Indians kidnap the hapless offspring of Christian settlers and raise them as their own, but I never thought I would be so fortunate as to meet such a specimen! Marshal Harkin, it would be my utmost pleasure—nay, my sacred duty!—to take this wretched, confused youth and instruct him in the ways of Christian brotherhood and make him a useful and productive member of society!"

Harkin shrugged. "If you want to take on the boy, that's your business, Reverend. Just make sure he stays out of trouble, y'hear?"

The Reverend Near's "church" was a shack placed on the farthest edge of town. The only thing that separated it from the other one-room shanties was a crudely-made whitewashed cross nailed over the front door like a horse shoe.

The church was one large room, divided in half by a couple of blankets suspended from a clothesline. The front half housed a couple of long benches and a wooden lecturing podium made from soap boxes.

"Welcome home, my son!" exclaimed Reverend Near, flipping back the room divider with an expansive gesture, revealing a pot-bellied stove, a table, a chair, a stool, and a narrow cot. Behind the stove, a built-in ladder lead to a half-loft.

As I stood and looked around, not quite certain what to do or say next, the Reverend pulled a black bag out from under the cot and began rummaging through its contents, still talking the whole time.

"What's your name again, boy? I didn't quite hear it the first time—?"

"Billy. Billy Skillet."

"An excellent name for such a fine figure of a young man! But first things first—before I can begin instructing you, we must get rid of these heathen adornments," he said, gesturing to my breechcloth and riding chaps. "A proper Christian gentleman doesn't parade around dressed like a wild Apache!"

"Comanche."

Reverend Near looked up from his black bag, peering at me over the tops of his smoked spectacles like an owl getting ready to snatch a mouse. "Never correct me, boy! The Lord says honor thy father and mother. And, as of this moment, you are now my son. At least in the spiritual sense. Is that understood?"

"Yes, Reverend." Actually, I *didn't* understand, but it seemed like the right thing for me to say. After all, I was new to the White Man's ways and I was in no position to judge what was right or wrong.

"Good. As long as you remember that, we should have no problems getting along," he said, his voice once again friendly as he pulled a large pair of scissors from the depths of his black bag. "Come here, Billy," he said, gesturing for me to draw closer.

I hesitated, my eyes fixed on the gleaming metal shears he held in his hand.

"You needn't fear me, my boy!" he laughed, showing too many

teeth for my liking. "I intend you no harm!"

Still uncertain, I took a timid step forward. The Reverend, scowling impatiently, suddenly got to his feet and grabbed me by one of my braids.

"I *said* `come here'! Are you deaf, boy?" he thundered.

Before I could reply, he neatly severed my right braid, taking it off level with my ear lobe. I yelped in alarm, clutching the side of my head as if mortally wounded.

"You needn't carry on so," the Reverend clucked, waving the scissors in front of my nose. "The way you're behaving, you'd think I was skinning you alive! Now sit down and let me tend to that remaining pigtail of the devil..."

I shook my head violently, backing towards the blanket that divided the living quarters.

"Billy, you're making your father very angry with you!" growled the Reverend. He'd removed his spectacles and I could see that his pupils were dilated as he came closer. I also noticed that he gave off a strange smell—one I would later identify as a patent medicine whose main ingredients were alcohol, bloodroot, and laudanum.

As I said before, the Reverend was a big man and, despite my status as a Comanche brave, I was still a youth of fourteen, and a rather slight one at that. While I had years of bareback riding and strenuous living on my side, the Reverend was a good six inches taller and outweighed me by at least fifty pounds.

Bellowing like a wounded bull buffalo, the Reverend grabbed me by hair and threw me roughly to the ground, planting his booted foot on the back of my neck.

Why did I not shapeshift, you ask? While I could have easily killed him in my true-skin, this was something I did not want. After all, it was my blood-lust that had driven me to seek the help of Whites in the first place. What good would it do me to make myself a pariah amongst them so soon? So I kept my human shape and took the punishment the Reverend meted out.

"Honor thy father and mother!" he shrieked as he worked to remove his belt. "I'll have no sassing' me in this house, young man! No back-talk! No misbehaving! You'll do as I say and like it!"

I winced as the belt came down across my bared buttocks, the buckle biting into my flesh, but refused to cry out in pain. It came down again—and again—and again—until my ass streamed blood, but still I remained silent. His rage apparently spent, the Reverend let the belt drop from his numbed fingers and staggered over to his cot, where he sat for a long moment, staring at me without seeming to see me.

"Sin no more," he mumbled, although I was uncertain whether this admonishment was actually directed at me. With that, he promptly closed his eyes and keeled over. He was snoring before his head touched the cot.

I slowly got to my feet, grimacing in pain. However, I knew my discomfort would be fleeting. I had discovered I possessed miraculous recuperative powers years ago, when me and a fellow brave were trampled by a wounded buffalo during one of the hunts. The brave died within hours of massive internal injuries, drowning in his own blood, while I was up and about the next day. More important than my physical state, however, was the situation I now found myself in.

I had suffered a humiliating physical insult that, in Comanche society, would have called for the death of my attacker if I was to reclaim my dignity. On the other hand, the Reverend Near, as far as I could discern, was a holy man of sorts, not unlike Medicine Dog. Which meant that he had access to hidden knowledge and was thereby worthy of respect. And it is well known that shamans of great power are often quite mad, prone to fits of violent, irrational behavior. And those who wish to learn from a shaman must suffer ritual debasement to prove themselves worthy...

I searched the room until I found the pair of scissors Reverend Near had abandoned during his frenzy. I looked at them for a long time, then at the Reverend, snoring away fully clothed on his cot. Then, without any hesitation, I reached up and snipped off my remaining braid.

My time with the Reverend lasted three months, and every moment remains vividly etched in my memory. For the longest time, I had no idea whether my so-called "spiritual father" was a holy man or a raving lunatic. Since I had nothing to compare White society against except the Comanche way of life, I was at something of a disadvantage.

During our frequent "tutoring sessions", which consisted of the Reverend reading aloud certain passages from the Bible and a pamphlet called "What Every Good Boy Should Know", two things were stressed: that it was a dire and mortal sin to touch oneself below the waist, and it was an even worse sin to have someone else touch you there.

The Reverend also advised against strong drink, calling it "the devil's blood". However, this prohibition did not extend to his own favorite beverage, a patent medicine called Mug-Wump Specific, which he guzzled at an alarming rate. I have no idea what, if anything, the potion was supposed to cure. But I soon learned that the Reverend's erratic behavior and violent outbursts were tied to his drinking it. Whenever the Reverend hit the Mug-Wump Specific, he would wander from his usual topics and rail against "tempting devils that appear as fair women" or the unfairness of life in general.

Gradually I came to know more and more about my new "spiritual father". I learned that his first name was Deuteronomy and that up until six months previous, he'd been the pastor of a respectable church in one of the wealthier neighborhoods in Chicago. I was never able to discover how he ended up in a reeking shit hole like Vermillion, but there was something about a young girl who had come to him to be taught her catechisms.

The Reverend claimed that the reason he was in Texas was to help bring the good news of the Lord and Savior, Jesus Christ, to the heathen Indians, and to provide spiritual guidance for the numerous cowboys, ranchers, and settlers working their way West. However, his attitude toward Vermillion was hardly charitable.

He had a low opinion of the members of his parish, reviling them as harlots, sinners, and ignorant barbarians. The reason for his acrimony stemmed from the town's steadfast refusal to acknowledge him as a pillar of its community.

I eventually came to know Vermillion's true opinion of the Reverend because he got into the habit of sending me on errands those days when he was feeling "poorly"—which was fairly regular. I would go alone to the general store to pick up his weekly supply of beans, bread, coffee, salt pork and Mug-Wump Specific, which gave me the chance to view the town and its inhabitants without the Reverend being around.

On my first solo journey to the store the Reverend lectured me at length on how important it was for me not to set eyes on the "palace of trollops", for fear of my mortal soul. Since the general store was two doors down from the saloon, it was hard for me to avoid seeing it, either coming or going.

As I was leaving the general store laden with groceries, I noticed Marshal Harkin seated in a bentwood rocker outside the saloon, rocking gently back and forth. Without missing a beat, he glanced over in my direction and beckoned me to come closer.

Although I was fearful the Reverend might be using the all-seeing eyes of God he was always talking about to keep track of my comings and goings, I was curious. Since my arrival in Vermillion the Reverend had kept me sequestered from its other citizens, assuring me it was for my own good, as the town was—in his own words—a "hotbed for all manner of sin and unnatural vice". I was to speak to no one, and this included Marshal Harkin, who was not only Vermillion's resident lawman, but also its pimp.

"You're that white indian boy the Reverend took in, ain't you?" he drawled, pushing back the brim of his derby.

"Yes, sir."

"He treatin' you good, boy?"

"Yes, sir."

"You look like a right enough young feller to me, Billy. Whenever you get your fill of hearin' about Jesus, you come see me. I'm looking for a boy to sweep up and empty the spittoons and slop jars. I'll pay you a dollar a week. Good hard cash. You think about it, hear?" He leaned forward and tucked a piece of candy into my pocket, winking broadly.

That was my first genuine introduction to Marshal Harkin, better known as "Gent" on account of his passion for fancy Eastern headgear. During my brief time in Vermillion, I would come to get to know him better than I would the Reverend.

Gent was an open, straight-forward cuss. He owned the Spread Eagle Saloon, where five rather tired-looking "dance hall girls" worked the clientele, taking them upstairs for two-dollar sex of the boots-on variety. He was fairly easy-going when it came to the cowboys who rode into town to let off steam during the round-up season. After all, they were his bread and butter. Gent was willing to overlook drunken cowpokes hurrahing the town—riding up and down the streets, firing six-shooters aimlessly into the air (and the occasional window)— but he was merciless when it came to saloon brawls. And more than one hapless cowboy found himself colder than clay after shorting one of Gent's girls.

On the whole, Gent saw the Reverend as a nuisance more than an upstanding member of the community. As far as he was concerned, the only reason anyone came to Texas was to get away from their past. The West was a place where a man could reinvent himself from the ground up without having to worry about phantoms from the old days coming back to haunt him. And it was clear to anyone with one eye and half-sense that the Reverend was hiding out from a damn big spook.

But the real reason Gent distrusted the Reverend was because he occasionally made forays into the Spread Eagle, attempting to sway the working girls from their lives of debauchery and sin. He had yet to win any converts, but Gent still took a dim view of anyone trying to stir up trouble in the hen-house. He knew Vermillion was still too young and poor to succumb to respectability, but he realized that it was only a matter of time before its citizens went from being rough-riding pioneers to civilized townspeople, and he sure as hell didn't like the idea of Reverend Near getting a jump on making Vermillion a decent place to raise your kids up.

He needn't have worried. Assuming Vermillion had a future at all, the Reverend was hardly destined to be its midwife. Besides, he didn't fool the whores one bit. They knew a sinner when they saw one. But not even they realized how bad off the Reverend really was.

Which leads me to the little girl. I don't recollect her name—it's possible I never knew it in the first place. All I remember is that she was one of the children that belonged to an immigrant sod-buster that lived on a farm just outside of town. Every now and then the Reverend would ride out there on his mule and try to convert the half-dozen or so families scattered about the countryside, but with little success. Most of them barely spoke enough English to buy seed and sell their eggs and butter, much less understand the gospel according to Deuteronomy Near.

The little girl disappeared one evening around supper time. Apparently a rather boisterous child by nature, she had talked out of turn at the dinner table, incurring the wrath of her parents. Her punishment was to stand on the front porch until the rest of the family had finished eating. When the mother got up to tell the little girl she could come back in, she was nowhere to be found.

At first they though she was playing a trick on them, but when several hours passed and the little girl still hadn't returned, the father rode into town and reported her disappearance, as best he could, to Marshal Harkin. Gent rounded up a search party. I asked the Reverend if I could help search for the missing child, but he refused to grant me permission.

When the first day of searching did not turn up any sign of the missing girl, Gent became convinced that one of two things had happened—that either she had been kidnapped by wild Indians or carried off by wolves, possibly even a bear. When the farmer translated the Marshal's suspicions to his wife, the poor woman became hysterical.

They found the little girl on the second day. After searching the surrounding gullies and washes, it turned out she was in her very own front yard.

They found her in the well. She had a burlap bag over her head and she was missing her knickers. The Marshal arrested the hired hand, who was a touch feeble-minded and got into trouble last season for fucking some of the livestock where the neighbors could see it. After a trial of sorts, they hung him. They never did find the little girl's knickers, though.

The Reverend, being the only man of the cloth in the county, officiated at the burial, even though the dirt farmers couldn't speak a lick of English and were probably Lutheran to boot. I was there to help officiate, although all I did was stand to one side of the Reverend and pretend to look sad. Since I didn't have anything else to do, I studied the grieving family.

The mother was a stout, round-faced woman who probably wasn't as old as she looked, her eyes red and swollen from crying. The father was tall and rawboned, his face unreadable as he tried to comfort his wife. His eyes remained fixed on his daughter's coffin, suspended over the open grave by a couple of planks. There were five other children, some older and some younger than the dead girl. One or two of them cried, but the others simply looked uncomfortable in their Sunday best, squirming and pulling at their starched collars.

After rambling on about innocence, sinners, lambs, Jesus and a better world beyond, the Reverend at last shut up and the grave diggers removed the planks, lowering the small coffin into the ground with looped ropes.

A week later I found the little girl's missing knickers wadded up and stuffed behind one of the loft rafters. They were stiff with dried blood and semen. I didn't know what to do about what I'd found—but I knew what it meant. It also decided something for me.

The only reason I'd put up with the Reverend's madness in the first place was the belief that he might have the wisdom to teach me how to control the killing wildness inside me. But now I knew for certain that the Reverend lacked the ability to curb even his own bestial tendencies, much less mine. That night, while he was passed out, I packed what few belongings I could call my own and trudged over to the Spread Eagle. Gent was playing solitaire in the saloon, a bottle of rotgut at his elbow and a foul-smelling hand-rolled dangling from his lower lip.

"So—you get enough Jesus, son?"

"Yes, sir. I come to see you about that job."

Gent grunted as he lay down another card. "Figgered you'd be comin' round sooner or later. I pay a dollar a week, plus what you can roll off the drunks. All yours, Billy."

"Thank you, sir!"

"Now get to work! I got slopjars that need scrubbin'!"

I must have scrubbed every slopjar in Vermillion that evening, and considering that most folks crapped in tin cans instead of porcelain chamber pots, that was probably a fair bet. After I finished with the slopjars, I had to clean and polish the spittoons, then sweep and mop the front saloon.

By the time midnight rolled around I was so tired I couldn't raise my arms over my head to take my shirt off. The bartender showed me my room—little more than a storage closet next to the back door, but at least there was a mattress on the floor. I'd been sleeping on nothing but dirty straw in the Reverend's half-loft, so it looked fairly ritzy. I collapsed into a sleep so deep I didn't even dream.

The next thing I knew there was a crashing sound coming from outside and the sound of a familiar voice raised in anger.

"Where is he?"

My eyes flew open and I had to fight to keep my fur from rising to the surface in self-defense. A growl slipped from between my clenched teeth.

"Where is that thankless heathen bastard?!?"

"Hey! What the hell do you think you're doin'?" yelled the bartender. "Somebody go fetch Gent! The Reverend's gone loco!"

The storage room door was jerked open and Reverend Near's frame filled the threshold. The stink of Mug-Wump Specific and madness radiated from him like heat from a flat rock. I scrambled to my feet to avoid being kicked in the ribs.

"There you are, you ungrateful piece of shit," he hissed. "I go to sleep for a few hours, and what do you do—? You turn on me and embrace mine enemies!" He shook his head sadly and for a moment it looked as if he was about to cry. "I thought I could save you, Billy. I really believed that God had a Plan for you. But now I was wrong—horribly wrong. You're just another sinner, given over to base fornication and intoxication!"

Sweat began to pour off my brow. Being so close to the Reverend's insane rage was making me twitch. If I didn't get out in the open soon, I would shapeshift involuntarily. I tried to move past the Reverend but he surged forward, grabbing me by the shirt-front, lifting my heels off the ground as he slammed me into the shelves lining the tiny room. His face was inches from my own, and one of the lenses in his smoked spectacles was cracked.

"Honor thy father!" he bellowed. *"Honor thy father, you little shit!"*

I lost control then—but only for a second. But it was enough. For the first time in months I let my bone and skin shift and twist, let the fur bristle and fangs sprout. And the Reverend Near suddenly found himself nose-to-muzzle with a snarling wolf.

He screamed in terror and let me drop. My butt coming into rough contact with the floor was shock enough to bring me back to my senses and I quickly reverted to my human self. The Reverend staggered backward, clutching his heart, his skin suddenly the color of tallow.

"Demon!" he gasped. *"Foul demon of hell!"*

"What in tarnation is goin' on here? Jesus on the cross, Reverend—didn't I tell you to keep outta my saloon?" It was Gent, looking blood-shot and none too happy to be ousted out of bed at such an ungodly hour as seven in the morning.

Before the Reverend could respond, Gent clamped a big, calloused hand on his collar and literally yanked him free of the storage room. The bartender and a couple of the girls peeped in to see if I was alive then hurried after Gent, who was frog-marching the Reverend towards the front door.

"You're harboring a fiend from the very Pit itself!" The Reverend warned, waving an arm in my direction. "A murdering beast that serves Satan as its master most high!"

"What the hell are you goin' on about *now*?"

"The boy! The boy is a minion of the Devil! I have seen him turn into a wild beast before my very eyes!"

"Go sleep it off, Reverend," Gent growled, delivering a swift kick to the raving minister's pants that propelled him through the saloon's swinging doors. Reverend Near fell into the thick muck that comprised Vermillion's main street, floundering and flailing like a drowning man. A couple of the whores had come out to see what the to-do was about and were having themselves a good laugh at the Reverend's expense.

"Trollops! Harlots! You shall not escape the Lord's judgement!" sputtered the Reverend, wiping the mire from his smoked glasses with as much dignity as he could bring to bear. Even though I knew the man to be a killer and a lunatic, I couldn't help but feel sorry for him.

"Come along, boy," Gent grumbled, leading me back into the dim interior of the Spread Eagle. "It's over."

I cast one last glance over my shoulder at the Reverend, struggling to extricate himself from the mud, and followed him inside.

Later that same day Gent arrested me for the murder of the little immigrant girl. I was sweeping up the front saloon when he walked up and, without any warning, pulled out his six-shooter and pressed its barrel right between my eyes.

"Hate to do this to you, son, but your under arrest."

Turns out the Reverend went home, got himself cleaned off, and returned with the pair of knickers I'd found up in the loft. They'd disappeared soon after I first discovered them, so I assumed the Reverend had burned them in the pot belly stove. Turns out he just moved them to a better hiding place.

The Reverend turned over the missing knickers to the Marshal, complete with a story about how *he'd* found them in *my* belongings the day after the little girl's funeral. Obviously, I had been tainted by years amongst the Comanche—I was no more than a murdering savage, inflamed by the sight of white woman flesh to the most horrific acts of rapine.

Gent hadn't been too thrilled on this key bit of evidence suddenly making its appearance—after all, he'd already hung a man for the crime— but the Reverend wasn't about to let this go by. So off to the pokey I went, manacled hand-and-foot.

Vermillion's "jail" was a airless adobe hut divided into two rooms. The front room, theoretically, was Gent's office, although he preferred lounging outside the Spread Eagle to spending time in that sweat-box. The second room was a tiny closet of a cell, with a wooden plank set on saw horses for a bed and a rusty coffee can for a slop jar. The one door was made out of iron with a trap at the bottom for meals to be pushed through, and there was a single narrow window set with bars. It stank of tobacco juice, vomit and old shit, since Gent rarely had occasion to use it for anything but a drunk tank, keeping rowdy cowboys in check until their trail bosses came to round them up.

As I sat on the rough plank, studying the heavy manacles that hung from my wrists and ankles, I realized my time as a citizen of Vermillion had reached its end. I knew what I had to do, and there was no joy in that knowledge. I had come to this place in hopes of learning how to tame the darkness in my heart, only to be forced farther from the light than before.

Shortly before dusk Gent pushed a dented tin plate of red beans and corn bread and a cup of cold coffee through the trap. He did not say anything, but I could feel him looking at me through the observation slit as I ate what was to be my last meal in Vermillion. I pushed the empty plate back through the slot and remained crouched by the door, listening to the clock-clock-clock of his boot-heels as he walked away, locking the front door behind him. I waited until it was well and truly dark before shapeshifting.

The heavy manacles dropped from my transformed wrists with a shake of my hands. I stepped out of my leg shackles, my paws scuffing the floor in ritual dismissal. I could have made a symbolic show of force by literally snapping the chains that bound me, but I had neither the time nor interest in such foolishness. Although my kind are stronger than a dozen men, our natural state is deceptively slight, with long, narrow hands and crooked legs that would make us seem ill-equipped for running at high speeds and bringing down prey with nothing but our claws and fangs. One should never rely on appearances.

Once transformed, it was relatively simple for me to yank the bars out of the window and squeeze myself through to freedom, leaving behind only empty manacles and my discarded clothes. The night was dark and windy, with lightning dancing on the far horizon. My pelt prickled and my nostrils twitched as I caught the scent of distant rain.

I slid through the shadows towards the edge of town, careful not to be seen during the brief stutters of lightning. I needn't have worried—most citizens were already sound asleep, and the few that were still awake were busy whoring, gambling, and drinking themselves insensate at the Spread Eagle.

The front door was unlocked—as usual—and the Reverend was passed-out, face down, at the kitchen table, an empty bottle of Mug-Wump Specific at his elbow. Next to the bottle of patent medicine was an open Bible and a pair of drawers. Judging from the color of the stains, this pair was considerably older than the ones he'd taken off the little immigrant girl.

The Reverend made a slurred grunting noise when I tickled his left ear with the point of my claws, then screamed like a woman when I tore it from his head. He sat up with a violent spasm that nearly sent his chair toppling backward. Without his left ear to support them, his smoked spectacles dropped away, revealing eyes bulging in their sockets like hard boiled eggs. He grabbed the Bible with a trembling, bloodied hand and held it as if he meant to swat me across the muzzle with it.

"Child of evil! I command thee; get back Satan!"

I snarled and knocked the book from his hand, grabbing him by the throat as I pulled him out of his chair. As I slowly crushed his windpipe, the Reverend opened his mouth wide, gasping for air. He issued a muffled shout, his body bowing upward, as I shoved the pair of knickers down his throat. The Reverend thrashed under my grip for several seconds, and although he was a very strong man, there was never a chance of him breaking free. And he knew it.

I left him there for the others to find—his mouth filled with a dead girl's underpants. No doubt the whores down at the saloon wouldn't be surprised.

I crept from the Reverend's shack, pausing to warily eye the approaching storm. Weather on the plains has a tendency to be sudden and violent, quickly metamorphosing into the fierce devil-winds the Mexicans called *tornado*. And something told me that was exactly what was brewing out on the prairie.

I stood there for a long second, studying the sorry cluster of buildings that comprised Vermillion. Pricking my ears forward, I could make out the Spread Eagle's piano in the distance, along with the occasional shriek of whore laughter. Maybe they knew there was a storm coming. Maybe not. Buffalo Face had been right. Whites *were* crazy, although some seemed crazier than others. Wherever the knowledge I needed to understand and contain my beast-nature might be, it certainly did not lie in Vermillion, Texas. I turned my back on the town and headed into the surrounding night.

Less than a hour later the storm caught up with me, pummeling me with hail the size of a child's fist. The wind was so fierce it knocked me down and kept me there, as if a giant hand was pressing me into the ground. I knew that if I remained in the open I ran the risk of being sucked into the storm—I'd seen a buffalo shoot into the sky like a stone from a sling a few seasons back. There was so much dust and dirt kicked up by the storm, it was impossible to see more than a foot in front of me, but I had the impression that the air above me was alive and angry, seething with raw power. Using all my strength, I crawled on my belly until I came to a dry river bed and rolled down the bank, pressing myself against the overhang for shelter. By this time the rain was coming down with such force it stung like nettles and jagged fingers of lightning tore at the night sky.

There was a distant rumbling that seemed to be growing closer, and at first I thought it was thunder—until I realized I wasn't hearing it, but feeling it through the soles of my feet. I looked up just in time to see a six-foot high wall of churning water, mud, and other detritus come rushing down the river bed in my direction. Even given my superior strength and speed, there was nothing I could do. The flash flood hit me with the force of a full-throttle steam engine, pulling me under and dragging me along as it raced towards nowhere. I surfaced once, long enough to glimpse a sliver of moon peeking through the heavy clouds, then the branch from an uprooted tree crashed into the side of my head and everything went dark.

CHAPTER FIVE

"**Y**ou dead, son?"

I peeled one eye open—which was fairly difficult, seeing how it was caked with dried mud—and looked up at a clear blue sky. I opened my mouth to speak but coughed up a lung full of dirty water instead.

"I reckon you ain't dead, then."

A pair of hands grabbed me under the armpits, levering me into a sitting position. Staring down at my mud-caked belly and genitals, I saw I was wearing my human body. A bottle was pressed to my cracked lips.

"Here, boy. Take a swig of this—good for what ails you."

I took a swallow. The liquid tasted like a cross between turpentine and gin and burned my throat. Coughing violently, I pushed the bottle away and vomited a mixture of river water and stomach acid.

"See? What'd I tell you?"

Wiping the grime and mud from my eyes, I finally got a good look at my benefactor. He was a short White man with muscular, slightly bowed legs and long, wavy brown hair that hung down past his shoulders. He was dressed in a stained and frayed linen suit that had once been white, a stovepipe hat perched atop his head. He was beardless and peered down at me through thick spectacles that made his eyes look grotesquely large.

Even with my limited experience of dealing with White society, I realized this man was not normal.

"W-who are you?"

The man in the once-white suit smiled and extended his hand. "The name's Praetorius! Professor Praetorius! And who might you be, young sir?"

I took his hand and allowed him to pump my aching arm vigorously. "Billy Skillet."

I slowly got to my feet, looking around me. I was standing on the bank of what was now a small river, surrounded by a tangle of driftwood, a dead cow made swollen and stiff from drowning, and other flotsam and jetsam left behind when the flood waters receded.

"I was scouting to see where the best place to ford the river might be," Praetorius explained, jerking a thumb toward the covered wagon waiting near the river bank a few dozen yards away. "That's when I found you. Weren't sure you was alive or not, seeing how you was completely coated in mud."

"W-where am I?"

"I reckon we're still in Texas. Yesterday I went through Vermillion, so you're twenty miles west of that..."

"Vermillion?" I eased myself down onto an uprooted tree that was now lying on its side, massaging my bruised skull. "You said you were in Vermillion?"

"What's left of it. Twister didn't leave nothin' but a greasy piece. Killed every white in town—no one left alive but a couple of Meskins. Had to leave. It don't pay to play to a crowd that small and that poor."

"Play? Are you an actor?"

Praetorius smiled again and tugged on his lapels. "Why, my good man—I'm in business! I sell my very own Patented Hard Luck Miracle Elixir! Guaranteed to cure neuralgia, cholera, rheumatism, paralysis, hip disease, measles, female complaints, necrosis, chronic abscesses, mercurial eruptions, epilepsy, scarlet fever, cancer, consumption, asthma, scrofula, diphtheria, malaria, and constipation! Good for both external and internal use!"

"Is it the same as Mug-Wump Specific?"

"Heavens no! My Patented Hard Luck Miracle Elixir is a thousand times more effacious!"

I grunted and got to my feet again, doing my best not to wobble. I felt like a shirt that's been beaten clean on a rock. Every muscle and joint ached and my guts were full of filthy water. Praetorius grabbed my elbow and helped steady me. As I said, he was somewhat short and I found myself eye-to-eye with his stovepipe hat.

"Dame Fortune led me to find you, Billy!" he said, steering me toward the covered wagon. I was too weak to argue and allowed him to lead the way. "Obviously, the Fates decided that it was not yet time for you to die—they knew you had work to do! Important work! They saved you from drowning in that horrible flash flood in order for you to help me!"

"Help you?"

"That's right, my boy! I've been in dire need of assistance. A partner, if you will. I lost my last help-mate a week or so back—poor Jack's horse stepped in a gopher hole and threw him." Praetorius put on a sad face and shook his head. "Broke his neck clean through."

"Sorry to hear it."

Praetorius shrugged. "No use crying over spilt milk, I say. Especially now that Providence has been so kind as to deliver you to me! Here, you sit in the shade next to the wagon while I go find you some clothes. We can't have you walkin' about with your johnson hangin' out."

Praetorius disappeared into the back of the wagon, where I could hear him shifting things about. I noticed there was what looked to be a cage of some kind fixed to the side of the wagon, balancing out the barrels of fresh water and supplies strapped to the other side. The cage was roughly four feet by four feet, protected from both the rays of the sun and prying eyes by a carefully draped tarp. Curious, I reached out and flipped back the canvas.

I don't know what I was expecting to be in the cage. Perhaps a wild animal of some kind. But I was definitely not prepared for what I did see.

There was a little man—at least I *think* it was male—about the size of a five year old child in the cage. He wore a rag over his loins and his twisted and stunted limbs were as filthy as any creature could possibly be and not be all dirt. He had a large, long nose that connected with the top of his small head without the interruption of a forehead, making it look as if his skull actually came to a point. This effect was magnified by his head being shaved except for a patch about two inches in diameter at the top, which was bound into a tiny knot with a piece of red yarn. The little man looked at me with permanently crossed eyes and smiled like an imbecile.

I took a couple of steps back from the cage and bumped into Praetorius. I had never seen anything like it before in my life. If a child was born with such deformities amongst the Comanche, it was immediately put to death. The Comanche way of life did not make allowances for those incapable of ever providing for themselves.

"What is it?" I asked, pointing at the little man in the cage.

"That's it," he smiled.

"That's what?"

"His name. Whatisit? He's my side attraction, in case no one's interested in a medicine show. I display him for a nickel a peek." He shoved an armload of old clothes at me. "Here, I found you some duds. Used t'belong to old Jack, rest his soul."

As I struggled into Praetorius' late partner's clothing, I couldn't take my eyes away from the creature in the cage. "Is it human?"

Praetorius opened up one of the provision coffers and took out some bread and an apple and passed it through the bars to Whatisit?, who chewed them with the complacency of livestock.

"Well, in the lecture I give the rubes, he's a man-monkey. `A most singular animal, which though it has many of the features and characteristics of both the human and brute, is not, apparently, either, but in appearance, a mixture of both—the connecting link between human and brute creation.'"

"Is that true?"

"Hell, no! But you can't tell people, `Now I've got this idiot here; take a good look at `im.' It's bad for business."

"He's not dangerous is he?"

"Poor Whatisit? don't have the brain-power to be mean," chuckled Praetorius, reaching between the bars to give the pinhead a scratch behind the ears. "Ain't that so, old fellow?"

Whatisit? giggled and, as if by answer, hurled a handful of shit at me, dirtying the front of my new shirt and splattering my chin.

"I thought you said he was harmless!" I snapped, brushing the idiot dung from my face and chest.

"No. I said he wasn't *dangerous*. There's a difference. `Sides, tossin' turds is his only vice. I can't deprive a man of his solitary pleasure, can I?"

And on that auspicious note, I began my tenure as a full partner in Professor Praetorius' Hard Luck Elixir Traveling Show.

As I said, the Professor was as crazy, in his own way, as the Reverend, but I liked him a lot more. Where the Reverend had been brooding and pensive, obsessed with sin and guilt and divine retribution, the Professor was interested in one thing and one thing only—making a dollar. He knew he was a con man and a charlatan and did not pretend to be respectable—at least with me. Another big difference between him and the Reverend was that while he pushed his patented cure-all on everyone from babies at the teat to old men with beards tucked in their belts, he himself never once put lips to it.

The Professor's way of making a living was unique, to say the least. Traveling from one pissant settlement to the next, peddling cure-alls to illiterate sod-busters and syphilitic townies, hardly guaranteed a steady or stable income, but it *was* exciting. And, in its own way, it reminded me of my boyhood, wandering from place to place. Every now and again we'd catch distant glimpses of Comanche hunting parties in pursuit of buffalo and antelope, but they never offered to come near us. I'd watch from the wagon, part of me aching as I wondered if my adopted father, Eight Clouds, or my old childhood friend, Quanah, was riding past.

But back to the medicine show. People didn't get much in the way of outside entertainment back then, so even the lamest of diversions was apt to draw a crowd and generate some interest. The Professor did business this way: we would camp well outside the city limits of his intended venue. Then he'd ride in and pay the sheriff a visit and offer him a dollar or three for permission to stage a show. If the sheriff wasn't agreeable, we'd set up shop just outside the town's dividing line and do it anyways. Then he'd hand a stray kid two bits to paste up handbills advertising Professor Praetorius' Hard Luck Elixir Traveling Show's imminent arrival, and give it a day or two for the news to percolate amongst the locals via word of mouth, then we'd ride into town.

Most of the Professor's wagon was taken up by a portable wooden stage he'd made special back in Philadelphia that was designed so it only took fifteen minutes to set up (a half-hour if it was raining), so the Professor could address the crowd from a platform almost as high as their heads without leaving the safety of the wagon. There were holes drilled in the stage so you could fix poles with banners stretched in between them that advertised the Hard Luck Elixir and Whatisit? One such banner read: *Prof. Praetorius' Hard Luck Elixir—Strong Medicine For The Weak-$1-Free To All Veterans Of The Revolutionary War.* (Seeing how this was the late 1850s, the Professor rarely had occasion to part with a free bottle of his precious snake-oil.)

The show would begin with me coming out onto the stage dressed in a bright-blue frock coat with a double row of brass buttons and shoulder epaulets, a pair of shiny Wellington boots, and a brushed beaver highhat with a bedraggled peacock feather tucked in its brim. (That last touch of theatricality virtually begged to be shot off my head—and was so, on more than one occasion.) I would then take up a drum and begin beating away on it, drawing a crowd as I did. Once the crowd was of a decent size, I would stop drumming and announce, as loudly as I could; "Ladies and Gentlemen! It is my honor to present to you the one! The only! The esteemed Professor Praetorius!"

The Professor, who'd been waiting inside the wagon behind a blanket curtain, would step out, accompanied by a drum roll. The Professor had a special white linen suit he kept stowed in a trunk and only wore for shows. He kept it clean by boiling it in so much starch it could damn near stand up on it own accord. At every show he'd present himself to the audience as an immaculate tower of medical knowledge, his elbows and knees crackling like dead leaves with every movement. (Of course the damned suit chafed like a bear and after each show, when the crowds had left and we were on our way to our next destination, the Professor would be busy smearing slave on his neck, johnson, and other tender parts that had been rubbed raw during his presentation.)

Watching the Professor work a crowd was a real education. He definitely knew how to talk a man into reaching into his pocket and handing over hard-won money for what amounted to rotgut whiskey mixed with horse liniment. I credit most of his success to his way with words. Only the Professor could get away with calling a simple glass of water "a chalice of Adam's ale". And for those unwilling to part with a dollar for a bottle of Hard Luck Elixir, there was always a nickel's worth of amazement in the form of Whatisit?

In order to lure the townies into surrendering their change, Praetorius puffed up Whatisit?'s pedigree from pinheaded imbecile to captured ape-man. To hear the Professor tell it, you were a cast-iron fool is you missed this chance of a lifetime to gaze upon such a unique specimen from Borneo, or Sumatra, or Tierra del Fuego, or wherever the hell the Professor decided Whatisit? was from that day. He made coughing up five red cents to stare at a caged freak sound not only educational, but morally uplifting to boot.

In order to show Whatisit?, the Professor rigged up a special canvas enclosure to one side of the stage large enough to allow up to ten to twenty people pass through at a time. Those foolish enough to crowd too close usually ended up splattered with pinhead shit, to the amusement of their fellows. It was my job to be sure that the line kept moving and that no one did anything to Whatisit?, like poke him with sticks or give him broken glass to play with.

After the Professor had finished his pitch and wrested what money he could out of the crowd, we'd pack up and get moving to the next stop as fast as possible. The Professor's official motto was "Always leave the customers happy", though the practical translation was closer to "Always leave them before they find out what they've really bought".

Although Whatisit? and I had gotten off on the wrong foot, I soon grew fond of the pinhead. As far as the Professor could tell, Whatisit? was probably in his late twenties, which was fairly old for a pinhead. By and large he was easy to control and wasn't hard to feed. The only time he got out of hand was when he had to be washed, but that wasn't often. Every now and again I'd take him out of his cage and put him on a leash so he could exercise, but he didn't seem to like being outside his box. He'd scuttle about on his hands and knees like a dog and make a high-pitched whining noise, occasionally clinging to my pants leg and walking semi-upright.

The Professor told me Whatisit?'s lack of enthusiasm for the outdoors was on account of his natural parents keeping him in what amounted to a crate ever since he was a baby, showing him at fairs and carnivals from the back of a wagon. They sold Whatisit? to the Professor in '49 in order to clear a debt. Whatisit?'s parents weren't too broke up over parting with their only son since they had a younger daughter with a parasitic twin who clog. (The daughter, not the parasitic twin.)

I traveled with the Professor for close to two years, tending the mules, mending the banners, walking and washing Whatisit?, decanting the foul-tasting Hard Luck Elixir into bottles and pasting labels on them. The elixir itself varied from brewing to brewing, depending on what the Professor could lay his hands on at the time. Often it was little more than watered-down rotgut, but I recall a couple of times when oil of turpentine, green vitriol, and sulphate of iron were tossed in to the mix—not to mention the occasional rattlesnake thrown in to give it extra "bite".

During the time we were together we traveled throughout most of Texas and into Oklahoma, putting on shows wherever there were enough folks with coins in their pockets to make an audience. As I stood on the stage before an endless parade of poverty-stricken farmers, illiterate ranchers, and pig-ignorant townies, each of them watching me, listening to my every word, memorizing every gesture and nuance so they could repeat it, verbatim, to their kin stuck on the homestead, I came to see myself through their eyes. I was no longer a skinny teenaged boy dressed in outlandish clothes that did not belong to him, but the herald of miracles, transformed by the glamour found in even the tattiest of traveling shows. It was the same magic that could turn a con man into the wisest of sages and a congenital idiot into a missing link from an nameless exotic land.

With all this folderol about cure-alls and tribes of monkey-men, no one knew—not even the Professor—that locked within me was a genuine miracle. I kept my condition to myself during my time with the traveling show, occasionally slipping away in the dead of night to hunt rabbits or howl at the moon. Once I shapeshifted in front of Whatisit?'s cage without checking to see if he was asleep first. Whatisit? frowned at me and sniffed the air, looking more confused than usual. When I reached between the bars to scratch behind his ears he whimpered and drew away. After that I made a point of waiting until I was several hundred yards away from the camp before changing.

As I said earlier, Professor Praetorius was careful to keep a step ahead of irate customers. We'd done our share of time in jail, here and there, none of it coming to more than a day or two at the most. But jail was actually the least of our concerns, since most towns we visited didn't even have proper law. What the Professor was worried about was angry customers showing up with a bucket of tar and a sack of feathers. And, as it turned out, when our time finally came, being tarred and feathered would have seemed like a pretty fair shake.

I don't recommend getting lynched.

Even for folks such as myself, who are notoriously difficult to kill, being hung is hardly a picnic. While a werewolf can't die of a broken neck, it *does* hurt like hell. Besides, if the person doing the lynching doesn't know what he's doing, instead of ending up with a snapped neck you'll get your head yanked off. And that'll kill *anything*, human or not. But I'm getting ahead of myself.

We were camped in the Oklahoma Territory, near the Red River. We spent a lot of time crossing the Red River in and out of Texas and Oklahoma. It tended to put off dissatisfied customers intent on reclaiming their money. Two days before we'd sold twenty bottles of Hard Luck Elixir in Turkey Creek, Texas, and the Professor had considered it prudent to cross back into Oklahoma. Just in case, mind you.

We were feeling pretty good about that little bit of salesmanship. So good, in fact, we'd elected to give ourselves a break and rest an extra day. We'd found a nice little campsite, sheltered by a copse of trees, with plenty of game nearby. It was spring and the wild flowers were in full bloom, carpeting the banks of the river for as far as the eye could see. It had been such a fine day I'd taken Whatisit? for a little walk, which he actually seemed to enjoy.

It was getting dark and the Professor and I were sitting by the campfire, eating supper. I reached out to pour myself some coffee, when there was this sound like the devil hacking into a spittoon and the coffee pot leapt four feet into the air.

"Put yore hands in the air and keep `em that way!" thundered a voice from somewhere in the trees.

The Professor and I did as we were told. A half-dozen men emerged from the surrounding twilight, each of them pointing a rifle in our direction. I recognized most of them as being members of the audience in Turkey Creek.

"What's the meaning of this?" The Professor demanded, doing his best to keep a waver out of his voice.

A tall, grizzled man in buckskin pants and shirt stepped forward and pointed his rifle square at the Professor's head. I knew right then these unhappy customers weren't going to be satisfied with just getting their money back.

"I'll tell you what the meaning of this is about, Mister Perfesser!" he snarled. "It's about how that elixir of yores poisoned my little gal!"

"That is unfortunate—but did you follow the direction on the label? I definitely draw a distinction between adult and child dosages—"

The grizzled man's face turned red as he cocked his rifle. "Shut up! I don't wanna hear no more of yore fancy talkin'! You done enough talkin' already!"

A second man, this one with watery eyes and carrying a burlap sack stepped forward. "Jed's girl ain't the only one you hurt, either! My Doris paid good money to see that freak of yores—we weren't home a hour when she went into labor! And look what she delivered me!" He took the sack and dumped its contents onto the ground in front of the

Professor. "You did this!" he sobbed, pointing at the stillborn pinhead. "This is yore doin'!"

The Professor's eyes narrowed at the sight of the tiny pinhead corpse. He licked his lips. "How much—how much do you want for it? With a little pure alcohol and formaldehyde—"

"You god-damn murderin' bastard!" shrieked the dead pinhead's father, catching the Professor square in the chest with his boot. "I'm gonna kick you yeller!"

The one called Jed grabbed him by the elbow and pulled him away. "Hold on, Ezra! Everyone here wants a piece of that sumbitch. And there's only one way we're gonna get satisfaction, and that's lynchin' 'em good and proper." Jed turned to look at me. "You pick yore friend up and stand were's we can see you. And don't try no funny business, y'hear?"

I nodded my understanding and went to help the Professor off the ground. He was bleeding from the nose and mouth and his spectacles were busted, causing him to squint so hard his eyes were slits. He shook his head and patted my hand.

"I'm sorry you're gonna die, Billy," he sighed. "I kinda always knew this would be how'd I leave this world. Goes with the territory. But you—you're a young man. Got your whole life ahead of you. Or did."

"Don't go talkin' like that, Professor. We can get outta this."

"My luck's played out, son. It's what I get for leavin' Jack to suffer the slings and arrows of outrageous fortune last time."

"Jack? Your old partner? I thought he died of a broken neck when his horse threw him."

"The broke neck part was true enough. But it was more on account of his horse being rode out from under him. I left Jack to hang in Burning Water, Texas, damn my soul. I make it a policy never to visit the same town twice, but it turns out some of Burning Water's citizens had moved there after losing a family member or two elsewhere. They recognized me when I rode into town to distribute fliers and followed me back to camp. They got the drop on Jack and I left him to them, curse me for the coward that I am!"

Before I had a chance to respond to what the Professor had confessed to me, there was a horrible shrieking noise from the direction of Whatisit?'s cage. One of the sodbusters had forced the lock and was trying to drag the terrified pinhead out. Judging from the shit dripping from his attacker's angry face, Whatisit? had already exhausted his only mode of defense.

The sight of the tiny, frail Whatisit?—frightened out of what little wits he possessed—shrieking and writhing helplessly in the grip of a rawboned cracker was enough to make me forget myself. "Leave him be!" I snarled, letting my teeth grow and hackle rise.

If any of the gathered farmers noticed the start of my transformation, I'll never know, because at the very moment I took my first step toward the struggling Whatisit?, Jed reversed his rifle and brought its butt down square on my head.

I woke up to find my hands tied behind my back, a noose around my neck, and a mule between my legs. They'd unharnessed the team that pulled our wagon; the Professor had his own mule, in deference to his position, while Whatisit? and I were forced to share the other.

The one called Jed squinted up at me, then at Whatisit?, shook his head and spat. He stepped back a couple of yards, cocking his rifle in preparation for firing.

"Any last words?" Jed asked the Professor.

"My one regret is that when I die, so dies my medical knowledge! Not since Hippocrates has there been such wisdom! What a loss to the ages—"

"To hell with you!" Jed bellowed, and fired the rifle.

The mules left in a right hurry.

At least Whatisit? and the Professor died quick. Their necks snapped like dry twigs. So did mine, for that matter, but I didn't die. Not that I felt good, mind you. Getting lynched, like I said earlier, is not my idea of entertainment. The first thing my body did was fill my pants, fore and aft, with shit and sperm.

Now, I've known folks who got their jollies from choking themselves, claiming orgasms on the brink of death are the ultimate in sex. I'd rather stick my dick into something living, personally. So there I was, jigging in mid-air, my eyes agog, my tongue stuck out, my lungs on fire, and my pants full of stuff I'd have rather kept inside me for awhile longer. The pain was so intense I couldn't concentrate long enough to shapeshift. (Not that it would have helped me any. If I'd succeeded in shifting right then, my so-called executioners would have filled me so full of holes it wouldn't have mattered that they didn't have silver bullets.)

As I struggled against the rope, it suddenly dawned on me that I better put my physical discomfort aside and play possum before one of the lynching party started feeling sorry for me and elected to put me out of my misery with a bullet in the brainpan. The moment I went limp, the lynching party issued a collective sigh and readied itself to leave. But before they left, they took the time to set the Professor's wagon ablaze—after they'd looted it and found the strongbox, of course.

As I slowly twisted in the midnight breeze, flanked on either side by a con man and a freak, I wondered just exactly where life was leading me and what was I expected to learn from this, my most recent experience. And, more importantly, I also wondered exactly how in hell was I going to get down?

CHAPTER SIX

There are a lot of things I've learned about being a werewolf over the years. And since I wasn't raised by my own kind, it's been something of a hard knocks education.

Most folks assume the only thing that can kill a werewolf is a silver bullet. That's true enough—up to a point. Silver *is* lethal to my kind, whether in the form of a bullet, blade or a bludgeon. But that's not the only thing that'll put us down. Like most living (or undead) things, being decapitated tends to slow us down. So does being burned alive. But outside of that, we're damn near indestructible. For instance, I discovered werewolves can grow back fingers, eyes, and other body parts the hard way. Which doesn't mean things don't *hurt*, mind you.

So there I was, dangling like some strange fruit from the limb of a cottonwood tree, my hands bound behind me and my neck snapped. Normally, most folks would be somewhat dead under such conditions. But not me. I was all too alive. Unfortunately, a snapped neck—while not fatal—was hardly a cold in the nose. It was going to take time for me to recover, and exactly *how* long I had no way of knowing.

As I was hanging there, I was extremely aware that the Professor and Whatisit? didn't smell so good. Not that either of them had been particularly aromatic to begin with. So it wasn't long before we attracted visitors.

Carrion crows, to be exact.

One of the bastards landed on my head, dug its talons into my scalp for a better grip, then leaned forward, so it was looking at me upside-down. It peered at me with one shiny black eye, then the other, trying to decide whether I was dead or not. Before I could muster a moan to scare the damn thing off, it flapped its wings and plunged its beak into my right eye.

There are no words that can convey what it felt like to have your eye skewered and yanked out of its socket. There were several excruciating minutes as the carrion crow worked to sever my optic nerve, yanking and pecking at it until it snapped. When the eye finally came free of its socket, the bird cawed out in victory, gobbling down its prize. Lucky for me, *vargr* meat is not very appetizing to beasts of the natural world, so it did not attempt to reach further into my skull and peck at my brains.

I spent the rest of the day twisting in the hot, dry Oklahoma wind and being tormented by every breed of fly known to man and beast which, unlike the crows and other scavengers, were not so particular in regard to taste. They were buzzing and biting and swarming about me in the hundreds. I could feel the little sons of bitches walking over my face, laying eggs in the corners of my eyes and in my nostrils. The idea of thousands of maggots chewing away on my face from within didn't improve my mood. By the time the sun went down I was one sorry, fly-bit son of a bitch, believe you me.

As the sun faded from the sky, I heard what sounded like a horse. I couldn't see who or what it was since I was dangling in the wrong direction. Next thing I know there is a black stallion with a rider dressed in clothes the color of midnight just a few feet from where I was hanging. The horse made a weird wickering noise and took a nervous side-step as its rider drew his gun and aimed it at me.

"Open your eyes, wolf-son," snarled the dark rider. Wherever he was from, it sure as hell wasn't Texas, judging from the thickness of his accent. "You can't fool me. I know you're not dead."

I lifted the lid from my remaining eye and glared at the stranger. "I can only open one. Damn bird ate the other one."

"They'll do that," grunted the dark rider, and fired his pistol point-blank, severing my noose just above my right ear.

I hit the ground and broke my shin, but compared to what I'd gone through that day, I didn't notice it. The dark rider climbed down from his horse and knelt beside me, using his knife to free my bound hands then rid me of my hemp necktie.

"You look like several miles of unpleasant road, as they so color-fully phrase it in this land," he laughed.

I squinted up at my savior with my left eye, more confused than grateful. "Who the hell are you?"

"My name is Saltykov, late of her serene highness, the Czarina Catherine II of Russia. But you can call me the Sundown Kid."

"Why?"

"Because I am a gunfighter, my friend! And all gunfighters have such colorful names! I find it most refreshing!"

I stared at the Sundown Kid for a long second. He was dressed like many of the cowboys I had seen—albeitly far more expensively. His black shirt looked to be made from silk instead of flannel, and he was wearing what looked like gold-plated spurs on his boots. He was young in the face, but not in the eyes or around the mouth. He was lean without being skinny, his skin so pale it seemed to glow in the moonlight.

"You're not human, are you," I said. "What are you then?"

He laughed for a second, then realized I wasn't joking. "You really don't know, do you? I shouldn't be surprised, I suppose. The *vargr* are notoriously lax when it comes to the education of their by-blows."

"*Vargr*?" That was the first time I'd heard the word. The sound of it made my ears prick, even in human form.

"Yes. That's the name for what you are. Just as *enkidu* is the name for what I am. Although some prefer the more vulgar human slang of 'werewolf' and 'vampire'."

I got to my feet, so excited by the immensity of my good luck I was close to both tears and laughter. The Sundown Kid clapped me on the shoulder and smiled, displaying pearly white fangs. "You better clean that eye out—you don't want a skull full of maggots, my friend," he said, gesturing at my exposed socket with his knife.

"Thank you for cutting me down! I owe you a great debt!"

"And I fully intend to have you make good on it. I am in great need of an *aide de camp*, you see. While I have devised an ingenious mode of protection for myself during the day, I still require the help of someone capable of functioning in open sunlight. My last servant came to a tragic end in New Orleans, and I have yet to find anyone to replace him. Until now."

"It would be my honor, Mr. Sundown Kid."

"Please—there is no need to be so formal. Call me Sundown."

In the two years since I left the Comanche to seek answers amongst the Whites, I had come across many different kinds of men; lawmen, badmen, madmen, and conmen. And now, with my introduction to the Sundown Kid, walking deadmen.

When Sundown told me he was a vampire, I had no idea what the hell he was talking about. As it was, I only had the vaguest notion of what a werewolf might be. I didn't want to let on just how ignorant I really was, so I kept my lip buttoned the first few days, although I was close to busting from curiosity. After all the time I had spent looking for someone who knew who and what I was, I was too tongue-tied to ask any questions!

Still, despite my initial ignorance, it didn't take me long to figure out that Sundown was a creature of dark and ancient power. He moved with the grace and strength of a wild animal, and when he spoke his words had the ring of one who is used to being obeyed without question.

While he could pass for human at a distance, up close it was obvious Sundown was far from your average shootist. His flesh was chill, like that of a corpse, his ears came to a slight point, and his wine-red eyes possessed cat-slit pupils. Like most of his kind, direct sunlight was something of a bother for Sundown. However, he had devised a unique method of keeping himself safe from the deadly ravages of the sun. He kept folded in one of his saddlebags what amounted to a cross between a shroud and a sleeping bag made of sturdy, but pliable, leather. Every morning, just before dawn, he would crawl into his portable coffin, fastening it shut from the inside with a series of buckles, and go to sleep.

The trouble was that while he was sealed inside, he couldn't travel and—worse yet—was vulnerable to discovery. That's where I came in. I rigged up a pony drag and hitched it to Sundown's horse, so it could haul its master during the day. Sundown was greatly pleased by my ingenuity. To show his appreciation for my abilities as a manservant, he allowed me to ride his stallion, Erebus, during the day instead of leading it.

It's hard for modern day humans to realize how big and empty this land was, even as late as the turn of the century. The eastern seaboard, like the European cities its denizens had fled, was over-crowded and densely populated. But in the days just prior to the Civil War, civilization ended with St. Louis, and from Kansas City on a man could travel for days—even weeks—without laying eyes on another human being—red, white or otherwise. It's easy to understand how folks came to see the West as a blank slate just waiting to be filled up with their dreams, expectations, and hopes.

And the Sundown Kid, like the hundreds of thousands of immigrant settlers who would stream across the prairies and badlands in the years to come, was looking to reinvent himself as well. During our travels together Sundown and I had numerous bull sessions. Sundown was a gregarious fellow and liked to talk about himself and the things he'd done and seen in the century since he fell prey to a vampire's kiss in Carpathia.

Essentially, Sundown was a romantic. He had the wanderlust and wearied of Europe during his hundred years of night-born immortality. He wanted to go somewhere new, somewhere fresh. Somewhere the locals didn't hang garlands of garlic and wolfsbane over their doors at night.

He had become friends with the American sailor John Paul Jones, who had come to Catherine the Great's court to serve as *Kontradmiral* during the war against the Turks. He was taken by the bold, straightforward seaman's manner and developed a fascination with Jones' native country.

I have yet to meet anyone who was more in love with the idea of America than Sundown. Granted, he spent most of his time draining the lifeblood of pioneers, settlers, Indians and cowboys, but his appreciation was heartfelt.

"While in Russia I became convinced that such a brash, new-born land would produce the freshest and most potent of nectars, free of the taint of in-breeding. I was correct! Even the sickliest rum-soaked derelict possesses the headiness of a fine claret!" he enthused.

I learned a lot from Sundown during our time together. He was an amiable and patient teacher, forgiving of my ignorance. He taught me most of what I know about the world that exists at the corner of humanity's eye, the societies that dwell in mankind's shadow, the races known as the Pretenders. And although he was not of my ilk, he knew enough about the *vargr* and their ways to answer most of my questions.

It was from him that I learned the name of my people and their history, albeitly tainted by the disdain that the *enkidu* hold for those Pretenders who must reproduce through the messy business of physical sex.

I learned that what I was, in truth, was a species of being known as a metamorph, a creature who could take the shape of both man and beast at will. I also learned that there are many different kinds of metamorph, scattered all over the globe. There were the *kitsune* of Asia, the *naga* of India, the *birskir* of the Arctic Circle, the *anube* of the Nile, the *bast* of Africa, the *silkie* and *undine* of the north and south seas... and the *vargr* of Europe.

The *vargr*, my particular clan, are wolves. And, according to Sundown, they were the most successful (meaning aggressive) breed of metamorph on earth. Europe had proven a fertile home for their packs, and many had come into power in the world of man as popes and kings and warlords, albeitly in human guise.

In fact, the *vargr* had proven so successful in getting what they wanted that they had grown bored with their original territory and begun traveling with their unwitting human cattle to the New World, often coming into conflict with the breeds of metamorphs and other Pretender races already established there. The *vargr*, like the Europeans they had tied themselves so closely to, were champion exploiters and imperialists.

"That is where I believe you originate from, my young friend," Sundance explained. "No doubt your sire was a *vargr* who came to this country in search of fresh pastures, intent on breeding his own pack. And, from what little you've told me, he was unfortunate enough to place his den too close to those familiar with the ways of the werewolf. Still, I must admire his courage in coming to this new world!

"While our peoples have warred with one another over dwindling territory and supplies in the Old Country, the *enkidu* have always held a grudging respect for the *vargr*. The *vargr* were the first of the Pretending kind to show interest in foreign soil, making them pioneers. And, in this strange and open country, I do not see any reason for such Old World animosities to continue. We are Pretenders together, wolf-son, surrounded by humans."

All of this information was heady stuff for a kid my age. Bear in mind, although I was almost seventeen years old (which is fairly young, even in human years) by *vargr* standards I was little more than a pup, still wet behind the ears with feet I had yet to grow into. For the first time in my life I began to think of myself as something besides a man. True, I had been aware of my difference, my *otherness*, from an early age. But I was raised human and taught to act human and respect the customs erected by humans. Still, there were some taboos I could not bring myself to knowingly break; the strongest of which was the deliberate taking of human life and the eating of human flesh.

About a week after Sundown and I first teamed up, we came across a small hunting party of Apache braves. There were four of them, huddled around a small campfire. Three slept wrapped in blankets while a fourth stood look-out. We watched them for a few minutes from atop a nearby rise, then Sundown climbed off his horse and began heading toward the camp.

"Where the hell do you think you're going?" I whispered.

"I'm going to go down and pay my respects."

"Are you mad? The Apaches don't like anyone who isn't Apache— and they *especially* hate Whites!" My warning was to no avail. By the time I'd finished my sentence Sundown was gone, swallowed up by the night.

Seconds later the Apache serving as look-out staggered backward, clutching his throat with one hand. As he stumbled backward, he succeeded in firing his gun once, but it was too late. Sundown flitted amongst the hapless Indians like the shadow of a bat, killing before they even had a chance to realize they were in danger.

I hurried down the side of the hill, still too stunned to do more than gape at the carnage in front of me. The smell of fresh blood was heavy in the night air, causing the dead Apaches' ponies to whinny nervously and paw the ground with their hooves. Sundown stood in the middle of the camp, his pale face dripping crimson. Now that the hard part was done, he was taking his time, going from body to body, draining the dead and dying warriors of their blood before it had a chance to coagulate.

"I saved you one," he grinned, gesturing to a butchered brave he had yet to drink from. "I know *vargr* like their kills fresh and juicy!"

I stared at the dead Apache for a long moment. My stomach growled and I began to salivate. Suddenly my mind was filled with the images of how I snatched poor Small Bear's liver from his bleeding carcass, and how I tore open Flood Moon's lovely soft throat with my bare hands, and I turned my eyes away from the freshly slain brave in self-disgust.

"Go ahead! What are you waiting for—?" asked Sundown as he knelt beside his second victim. "They don't get any better with age, my friend!"

"I'm not hungry." It was a lie. My stomach was growling like a sore bear, but I could not bring myself to knowingly partake of human flesh.

Sundown shrugged his indifference and resumed his feeding. "More for me, then."

It was only a few days later that we came across the Comanche. It was daylight and I was riding Erebus, leading one of the ponies we'd taken from the Apache camp. I saw them framed against the horizon. Although they were too far away for me to make out their clan, I knew they were following the buffalo, gradually making their way towards the Brazos River.

I reigned Erebus to a halt and watched the cloud of dust rise stirred up by the hooves of the hundreds of ponies herded by the young boys of the tribe. So many horses together was a sign that this was a wealthy clan, one that had won many ponies through successful raids against the Whites, Spanish, and other Indian tribes.

A handful of braves broke off from the main group and headed my way, whooping and waving their lances and shields, but I did not move.

As they approached, I recognized their clan-markings as being those of the *Penateka*, my old tribe.

The braves were young and fierce, eager to show their contempt for Whites. They rode their ponies around me in a tight circle, giving vent to war-cries that would have chilled the blood of a true White Man. I sat quietly on my mount, watching them impassively. After a minute or two of shrieking and waving rifles and war-axes at me, they fell back and a young warrior rode forward. Although he could have been no older than myself, his hair was already plaited with the eagle-feather of a sub-chief.

At the sight of the grim-faced Comanche I suddenly grinned and lifted my hand in ritual greeting and called out in their tongue, "Good day, Quanah!"

The sub-chief seemed taken aback and blinked, frowning uncertainly. His eyes narrowed as he studied my face, only to widen in recognition a moment later.

"Walking Wolf! My brother!"

Laughing loudly, we climbed down off our mounts and embraced in front of the perplexed young braves. After a few moments of pounding each other's backs, Quanah turned to his fellows and pointed at me.

"This is my brother, Walking Wolf! The one I had thought lost to me!"

The braves muttered amongst themselves and I could tell by the looks that passed between them that stories of my being the living hand of Coyote were still being circulated around the campfires.

"How have you been, Quanah? Is you father, Peta Nocoma, well?"

At the mention of his father's name, Quanah's face darkened. "My father is dead. The season after you disappeared, Rangers came and stole my mother and baby sister from the camp. Peta Nocoma tried to stop them, but it was no good. He died in the Antelope Hills from the wounds the Rangers gave him as he fought to save his wife."

"That's a shame, Quanah. Peta Nocoma was a good chief. What of Eight Clouds Rising? Is he well?"

Again Quanah shook his head. "He died of the White Man's pox last season, along with Little Dove and many others in the tribe."

Now it was my turn to look sad. Eight Clouds might not have made me, but in all the ways that counted, he had been my father.

One of the braves called out to Quanah, pointing in the direction of the main body of the tribe. A young boy riding a spotted pony pulling a drag was coming our way. Quanah smiled and turned back to me.

"It looks like Medicine Dog has seen your return, Walking Wolf."

"Medicine Dog? He's still alive?"

"The Great Spirit will not allow him to die, at least that is what he claims," Quanah said with a shrug.

The pony drew up beside me and I could see the withered form of my old teacher huddled on the litter, wrapped in blankets like a grandmother. He turned his ancient face toward me and spoke.

"Greetings, Walking Wolf. You have been a long time gone."

As I stepped forward to reply, I could tell that the old shaman's remaining eye has joined its twin in darkness. "Greetings, Medicine Dog. It is good to see you."

"It is good to see you too, Walking Wolf. Although I see you with the eyes of my heart, not with the shrivelled things in my head."

"How are you, Medicine Dog? Do you still counsel the tribe?"

The old man shrugged. "In some things I am consulted. The older ones still come to me for advice. More and more the younger ones turn to Coyote Shit in such matters."

"Coyote Shit?" I couldn't believe my ears. I'd known Coyote Shit from when we were boys—he was always coming up with hare-brained schemes that ended up landing those foolish enough to go along with him in trouble. Perhaps the years had changed him, but I doubted he had half the vision with two good eyes that Medicine Dog had with none.

"You sound surprised, my son," Medicine Dog said, a sly smile on his lips. "Do you doubt Coyote Shit's ability?"

"The *Penateka* is making a mistake."

"Perhaps. You shall be able to judge for yourself in a moment or two. Coyote Shit is coming."

I glanced up and sure enough, there he was, riding toward the little band gathered around my horse. He looked pissed. Someone must have told him that old Medicine Dog had gone out to join Quanah. I'll give him one thing—he knew how to make a show of it; he hopped off his horse without waiting for it to come to a full stop and pointed his coupstick at me and thundered; "The White devil brings evil medicine!"

Quanah—who always had a low tolerance for Coyote Shit's antics when we were boys—rolled his eyes. "This is not a White devil, this is my brother, Walking Wolf."

Coyote Shit's face darkened as the other braves laughed. "That may be so, but I say he carries bad medicine! If you doubt my word, ask the old man."

Quanah looked to Medicine Dog, shrouded in his blankets. "Does he speak truly?"

Medicine Dog nodded. "Coyote Shit does not lie. Walking Wolf carries death with him."

Coyote Shit pointed to Sundown's leather sleeping shroud, lashed to the pony drag hitched to Erebus. "The evil lies in here!"

Quanah looked at me inquisitively. It was now up to me to explain myself. I decided to come clean.

"I carry with me a White Man who is dead during the day and walks at night. He drinks the blood of the living—both animal and man. He hunts them as you hunt the buffalo, in order that he might survive. He is very old and very wise, in his way. I wish to learn from him—but to do so, I must serve him in this fashion."

Quanah eyed the leather bag, obviously trying to decide whether or not he should do something about its contents. "This living dead man—does he drink the blood of the Comanche?"

"He claims to prefer the blood of settlers."

Quanah mulled this over for a long second. "Then I guess it is none of our business. If this dead man only drinks the blood of our enemies, we have nothing to fear."

I glimpsed Coyote Shit, out of the corner of my eye, hunkering down and poking at the leather shroud with his coup-stick, as if trying to raise hornets from a nest.

"Stay away!" I snapped, allowing my *vargr* face to surface for a heartbeat. Coyote Shit yelped in alarm and scuttled backward on his hands and heels. I could tell, first by the look on his face, then by the smell, that he had soiled himself. This amused the assembled braves, who had a good laugh at Coyote Shit's expense.

His face burning with shame, the young medicine man strode back to his mount, doing his best to maintain some semblance of dignity admist the laughs and cat-calls. If I hadn't known him to be a pompous fool with delusions of grandeur, I might have felt sorry for him.

"I must go, Quanah. I have far to go. And I do not want to be close to where the Wasp Riders will make camp when it grows dark."

Quanah grunted and nodded. "Perhaps you will return to us some other day."

"Perhaps."

With that, my old friend hopped back on his pony and lead his band of braves back in the direction of the tribe. Only Medicine Dog remained.

"So—what do you think of Coyote Shit, now that he is grown?" he asked.

"The man's a fool!"

Medicine Dog shrugged. "Perhaps he is a holy fool. All I know is that the tribe would rather heed his words than mine." Medicine Dog pulled a leather pouch out of the tangle of blankets and shook it. I recognized the dry rattle of thunderstones—the fossilized bones of the great beasts that once wandered the plains in the time before the White Man even dreamed of this land. Medicine Dog was looking into the future. "Coyote Shit sees but little. He is a small man who would walk in big shoes. What vision he has is dim, and he is too proud to allow his sight to grow. And in the end, his medicine will be false. He will lead the Comanche into the killing coral. Not within my lifetime. But soon."

"And what about me? What do the thunderstones say about me?"

Medicine Dog stopped shaking the bag and shrugged. He frowned and his withered eyes seemed to grow moist. "They say you still have much to learn. Much to see. Much to suffer. And they say you will not see me again. Goodbye, Walking Wolf."

"Goodbye, grandfather."

The boy astride the pony clucked his tongue and it started away, hurrying to rejoin the others. I watched the old blind man sitting stiffly on the drag, facing backward, clinging to it as he was pulled across the plains, until he was swallowed by the dust on the horizon.

He was right. I never saw him again.

At least alive.

CHAPTER SEVEN

I met the devil at Pilate's Basin in 1861.

I don't mean the kind of devil you see wearing red long johns and horns with a pointy tail and a pitchfork. No, this devil was more *real* than that. More *personal*. He was my very own private demon.

I'd been travelling with Sundown for close to a year by the time we made it to the high plains of what is now Colorado and Kansas. The high plains is an arid stretch of nowhere that would make God Himself cuss Creation. A fine, crystalline snow swirled endlessly in the high wind, making it a lot like being rubbed down with a piece of sandpaper. I couldn't speak without making my lips bleed, I was so freeze-dried.

The sky was perpetually overcast and sometimes the only way I could tell whether it was day or night was by Sundown climbing in and out of his shroud. It was late fall, heading into winter, and the days were growing shorter and the nights longer, so Sundown was spending more and more time out of his traveling shroud. Not that this did us much good—you could go weeks out there without seeing another soul, human or otherwise. As it was, we'd already sacrificed my horse to feed the both of us.

Nonhuman or not, I knew that if we didn't find some real shelter soon, Sundown and I stood a good chance of dying like any other poor bastard who gets himself lost in the trackless wastes.

That's when we came across Pilate's Basin.

It wasn't a town—not the way most folks picture one, leastwise. It was a cluster of adobe buildings—no more than large huts, really—huddled against the wind. The warm, yellow glow of lantern light seeped out from the main building's shutters, along with a thin spume of smoke.

I knocked on the door with cold-numbed knuckles, not sure what to expect from whoever might live inside. There was the sound of a bolt being thrown back and the door opened.

"Come on in, stranger! And be quick about it! I don't want the wind puttin' out my fire!"

I hurried inside and the door was quickly slammed behind me. The inside of the adobe was close and warm, but surprisingly neat. As I turned to thank my host, I caught a glimpse of what looked to be a shrine of some sort next to a narrow cot. A woman's lace shawl covered a crudely built table on which were set a couple of tallow candles placed in saucers, illuminating a faded and dog-eared rotogravure of a dark-haired, dark-eyed woman dressed in the black lace mantilla of a Mexican *señorita*.

Standing next to it was a man who was either thirty or eighty—it was hard to tell by his face, which had been severely weathered by the winds and harsh climate of the plains. Had he been without teeth, he would have resembled one of the dried-apple dolls children played with. Although his face looked prematurely aged, my host was powerfully built, with wide shoulders and big, callused hands.

"The name's McCarthy. Who might you be, stranger?" he said.

"Skillet. Billy Skillet."

This seemed to amuse him and he smiled, "Is that a fact? Well, Billy Skillet, why don't you go put up your poor horse before it freezes, eh? The stable's around back. When you're done, you can join me by the fire for a chat."

"Sounds mighty good to me."

I lead Erebus around the back of the adobe and put him inside the stable, quickly hiding Sundown's shroud under a mound of hay. I then unhitched the pony drag and unsaddled the horse. As I worked, McCarthy's own horses watched me nervously. Like most animals, they knew an unnatural thing when they smelled it.

By the time I made it back to the main hut, McCarthy was already seated in front of the open hearth, sipping coffee from a tin cup. "Brewed you some mud," he said, pointing to a second dented cup sitting on the table. It was black as goddamn and had a bite like a rattlesnake.

"That's damn good coffee!" I said through my teeth.

"Set yourself down and warm your stumps, Billy," he said, gesturing for me to sit on a stool placed next to the hearth.

I did so and, without much in the way of prompting or preliminaries, McCarthy set about telling me the story of how he came to be stuck in the "devil's bunghole," as he put it.

"My parents came to this country from Scotland. They started out in Baltimore—that's where I was born. My father worked as a clerk in a bank, tending other folks' money every day of his life, bless him.

"Me, I never had much love for banks, or working jobs that killed a man from the inside out. I was the adventurous type. So I hired on with the U.S. Navy. I was a good enough sailor—until the day my captain ordered me striped for insubordination. I didn't take to having the cat on my back, that's certain. So I jumped ship—deserted, if you will—and ended up in Mexico. I met a lovely young woman there"—his eyes flickered over to the shrine beside the door—"and I fell in love with her. And she with me. Her family did not approve, however, since I was nothing but a lowly *gringo*. What could I possibly offer her?

"They were right and I knew it. I guess I could have put the pressure on Carmelita—that was her name—and had her insist on having me as her husband, but I was proud. I wanted to *prove* to both her and her family that I was sincere—that I was something beside an opportunistic *yanquis.* So I agreed to work for her family, who had considerable land both in Mexico and America.

"Her family used my willingness to serve them by sending me to the farthest reaches of their holdings, to oversee their herds on the high plains and operate a trading outpost. It was their way of washing their hands of me without resorting to killing me themselves. That's why I call this place Pilate's Basin.

"I've been out here close to ten years. During that time I've turned my place of exile into an unofficial traveler's rest for those who come my way. All I ask in way of payment is news of the outside world."

"What about the girl—Carmelita?" I asked, warming my hands as I spoke.

McCarthy smiled sadly and sighed. "She was very young. Younger than me by a few years, at least. After a couple of months, perhaps a year, she forgot about me. She ended up marrying some fellow her family approved of. I didn't know about it until I'd been out here, oh, six or seven years. By that time she'd had a couple of young'uns and was fat as mud— or so I was told."

"If she went and married someone else, why are you still stuck out here?"

McCarthy shrugged. "I'd gotten used to it, I reckon. Even though it can be mighty lonesome out on the high plains, least I'm my own boss out here. There ain't anybody to beat me or order me around. After all this time, I probably wouldn't know how to deal with a town full of people, all running around and getting into each other's business."

I found myself liking McCarthy, who had willingly exiled himself for the love of a fickle young girl. It was a shame he was going to die.

McCarthy got up to prod the fire with a poker as a particularly strong gust of wind slammed against the hut, rattling the shutters. He glanced in the direction of the door, as if expecting it to open. "It'll be dark soon. I hope that fellow didn't get lost out there."

"Fellow? What fellow?" I said, my scalp tightening. For a second I imagined McCarthy knew about Sundown and our plans to ambush him.

"Another traveler, such as yourself, that's all. He showed up a couple of days ago, just as the storm was getting ready to hit. He goes by the name of Jones. But don't they all? He headed out a few hours ago to look for some game. Hope he can find his way back."

As if on cue, there was the sound of heavy boots on the front porch and the front door swung open, letting in a chill blast of air. I turned around to get a look at McCarthy's house guest, and that's when I set eyes on my private demon for the first time.

He was huge, covered with hair, and had two heads—one of which was horned. Then I realized I was staring at a man dressed in a full-length buffalo skin coat with a dead antelope tossed over one shoulder. He stepped inside the house and slammed the door shut behind him, shrugging the antelope onto the floor as if it was a woman's stole.

McCarthy bent over the carcass, shaking his head in awe. "I didn't believe you when you said you'd bring back venison! But, by damn, you done it!"

Jones removed his heavy buffalo-skin coat and tossed it in the corner. Underneath the coat he was wearing a shirt made from what looked to be timber wolf or coyote skin. This he did not offer to remove.

"Hunting is in my blood." His voice was deep, like that of a pipe organ, with a slight Slavic accent. As he turned to face me, I was struck by his bristling beard the color of McCarthy's coffee, which seemed to start at his cheekbones, and eyebrows so thick and bushy they literally covered his brow-ridge from temple to temple.

Jones fixed me with piercing eyes the color of a coming storm and scowled. "I saw a strange horse in the manger. Who are you?"

Before I could answer, McCarthy piped in; "This here's Billy Skillet. He showed up just an hour or two back. Got himself lost in the storm..."

"Have we met before?" he asked, staring at me even harder.

"I don't think so."

Jones grunted and brushed past me to stand in front of the fire. As he warmed his hands and stomped his feet to restore circulation, I found myself staring at his wolf-fur jacket. There was something...familiar about it. Something I couldn't place. Maybe I *had* met this hairy-faced giant before. Perhaps he was one of Professor Praetorius' erstwhile customers.

"That's a fine shirt you got there, mister. How many wolves did you have to kill for it?"

"Just one."

"Must have been a damn big wolf!" McCarthy snorted.

"It was. Big as a man."

I cleared my throat. "Excuse me, sir. I don't believe I caught your name...?"

"They call me Jones." The giant didn't even dignify me by glancing in my direction.

"Jones? Is that all?"

There was a pause, as if he was deciding on whether or not to reply, then he slowly turned his head and fixed me with those gray eyes and said, "Witchfinder. Witchfinder Jones."

"Unusual handle. How you come by it?"

The big man returned his gaze to the fire. "I hunt things."

"What kind of things?"

"I hunt *things*. Vampires. Witches. Warlocks. Ghosts. Werewolves."

"That's plum silly! There ain't no such things! Ain't that right, McCarthy?" I laughed nervously, glancing over at the older man for support.

However, McCarthy was shaking his head. "I wouldn't say that, Billy. I seen a lot of things that couldn't be explained, both here and when I was at sea. Snakes with wings, women with the tails of fish, serpents that chased down and ate killer whales..."

I was starting to feel dizzy. There was a scent rising from Jones' jacket as the frost clinging to it melted away. I found myself needing to sit down. I looked over at McCarthy, to see if he'd noticed, but he was busy hacking off one of the antelope's haunches with a cleaver in order to prepare the night's meal. The smell of the animal's blood made my stomach knot with hunger. It'd been a couple of days since I'd finished the last of my old horse.

With a deep, guttural sound, almost a growl, Jones lowered himself onto a chair next to the fire. Without looking at me, he fished a hand-carved briarwood pipe and a drawstring pouch out off his wolf-skin shirt. For some reason I could not take my eyes from the leather sack that held his tobacco.

"That's—um—a mighty unusual tobacco pouch you got there."

Jones smiled then—it was an ugly sight, believe me. "This is the only one of its kind. It is a trophy. Just like my shirt." He leaned forward and held the pouch out to me. As if in a daze, I reached out and took it. Some faint memory squirmed in the back of my brain like a blind grub. A memory of warmth, the smell of flesh, the taste of milk...

"I took the pelt for my shirt off a werewolf seventeen years ago...just as I took his mate's left tit for a tobacco pouch. I keep the whore's vulva in a box in my saddle-bag...salted, of course."

I stared at my ma's breast, trying to summon further memories beyond those of a blind, suckling pup—but none came. I looked up at the man responsible for the slaughter of my family, meeting and holding his gaze. Although I realized he knew what—if not who—I was, I refused to let him rattle me.

"What you say is all very well and good," I remarked, handing back what remained of my ma's breast to her murderer. "But how am I to know you're not just flat-out crazy? For all I know, you took that off some poor Indian gal. And as for the shirt—well, a wolf skin is a wolf skin."

Jones shrugged his indifference. "It doesn't matter to me if you believe me or not. I know what I know. I do what I do." He produced a buck-knife, its blade shining in the light from the fire. It was silver. "I use my knife and I use my silver bullets. Nothing unnatural can survive a wound dealt by silver. There are plenty who believe me—and pay me to rid them of these monsters."

"Is that what you're doing out in the middle of nowhere? Hunting monsters?"

Jones re-sheathed the knife and turned back to the fire. "I was hired to kill a vampire."

I felt my stomach hitch itself even tighter. "Vampire?"

"Aye. One I have been tracking since New Orleans. There was a young girl the creature—outraged—in the city of Boston. Her family is of some stature, and they hired me to track the fiend down and bring back his head. I first found him in New Orleans, in a fancy Basin Street whorehouse. I would have claimed my bounty then, except for the interference of his servant. The bastard shot me in the shoulder. It wasn't much of a wound, really, but it was enough to make me lose my prey. I dealt with the manservant, though. I put the silver bullet I had reserved for his master right between his eyes."

Jones was describing the demise of my predecessor. The knowledge made the sweat rise on my brow and upper lip.

"It took me a couple of days to recover from my wound, but by then the fiend had fled the city. He had a head start, but not enough of one that I could not track him. I have since seen evidence of his passing: Indian raiding parties slaughtered to the man as they tended their campfires; isolated farm houses where the family members were drained white at the dinner table; hotels where, after the stranger checked in for the night, half the residents were found dead in their beds the next morning.

"Somewhere along the line the monster found someone else to serve him. Someone to hide and transport his body during the daylight hours.

Someone else to help him do his dirty work... Or should I say, some *thing*?"

He was staring at me, the storm clouds in his eyes looking as if they were about to break. I could tell by his body language he was getting ready to lunge at me. I knew I should try to get up, move away from him, prepare my own counter-attack, but my dizziness had grown worse. Sweat was pouring down my back and my head ached horribly.

Witchfinder Jones leaned even closer, until his hairy face was inches from my own. His wide nostrils flared like those of an animal scenting blood. "I can *smell* an unnatural thing from a mile away, boy."

Before I had a chance to respond, there was the sound of something heavy striking meat and Jones' eyes rolled up in their sockets and he pitched sideways out of his chair, narrowly missing landing in the open fire. I stared for a long moment at the big man sprawled on the floor, a halo of blood forming about his skull, then turned to look up at McCarthy, who stood over the body, a hammer clutched in one hand.

McCarthy's eyes gleamed strangely in the light from the fire. They reminded me, in a way, of Sundown's eyes when he got the hunger on him.

"Had to wait him out. Wait until he wasn't paying so much attention to *me* and what *I* was doin'." McCarthy rubbed at his mouth with his sleeve. "Tried slippin' the stuff in his coffee the first night, like I did with you, but he was too big. Too tough. It didn't take."

"Wh-what did you do—?" I tried to get up from where I was sitting, but my legs gave out and I found myself on the floor. McCarthy squatted down next to me, peering down into my face.

"I don't like using force. Usually I just dose their coffee, then they go to sleep and don't feel nothing—not even when I brain 'em with the hammer. But this one—and you, for that matter—just ain't respondin' properly. I hate it when that happens. I don't like using violence. I'm a peaceable man, by nature."

I tried to change then, to slip from my human form into my faster, stronger *vargr* skin, but I couldn't focus. The room was swimming and everything seemed to be pulsing with a rhythm all its own. I watched, helpless, as McCarthy raised his hammer on high.

There was a rush of cold air and something black struck McCarthy head-on, knocking him backwards. I heard the exile scream as my savior tore into his throat. I didn't feel so sorry for McCarthy anymore.

The next thing I knew Sundown, his mouth wet with fresh blood, was helping me to my feet. "You alright, Billy?"

"He—he must have drugged me..." was all I could mumble.

"He put enough laudanum in your drink to kill a normal human three times over. I woke shortly after you placed me in the stable. I decided to check the other buildings, in case there were more humans about. There are. But they are all dead. There must be over a dozen corpses stashed in the out-buildings, all in various stages of decay. I'd say the oldest was five years old." Sundown shook his head in disgust. "Humans! And they accuse us of being monsters! But at least the mad man did us the favor of ridding us of that wretched bounty hunter!"

A groaning sound came from the direction of Jones' body. Sundown and I stared, open-mouthed, as Witchfinder Jones sat up. His hair and beard were sodden with blood, and part of his brain bulged outward through the crack in his head. His left eye was so full of blood it leaked from the corners like crimson tears. His right eye was as clear as before—only angrier.

"I got you now, you stinking whore-son!" the bounty hunter bellowed, pulling out a revolver.

"Run, Billy!" Sundown yelled, propelling me towards the open door. "Run!"

I stumbled forward, my limbs still numb from whatever drug McCarthy had slipped me. I turned to see what was happening, only to slam into Sundown just as Jones released his initial volley.

The first shot went wild of its target. The second did not. Sundown opened his mouth and vented an ultra-sonic shriek of pain. I caught my friend as he pitched forward and dragged him out of the hut as Jones struggled to get to his feet, his boots slipping in a pool of his own blood.

I didn't look at Sundown or ask him if he was okay. I was too scared to do anything but run with him to the stable, where—reverting to my boyhood—I hopped on Erebus bareback and simply fled, clinging to the horse's neck with my right arm while I cradled Sundown to my breast with my left. As we charged past the front of McCarthy's hut, I glimpsed Witchfinder Jones slumped in the doorway, taking aim at me. I dug my heels deep into Erebus' flanks just as a silver bullet whizzed past my ear. I heard Jones bellow something into the storm that might have been a name, but it was quickly snatched up by the wind and made meaningless.

It was close to a half-hour later before I was willing to slow my pace enough to check on Sundown's condition. I had him pressed between me and the horse's neck to keep him from falling off.

"Sundown? Sundown—? Are you alright?"

No answer.

"Saltykov?" I said, hoping he wasn't in such a bad way that he would not respond to his true name.

No answer.

I touched my friend's shoulder gingerly, hoping to rouse him enough to at least groan. To my horror, I felt the bone and flesh inside his shirt crumble at my touch.

I howled as the wind caught the dust that had, until a few minutes ago, been my friend and tossed it skyward. I howled for my father, whose pelt now covered his killer's back. I howled for my mother, whose breast now served to carry her murderer's tobacco. I howled for my friend, now reduced to nothing but flakes of decayed skin and powdered bone. But most of all, I howled for myself, lost in the wilderness.

CHAPTER EIGHT

After the death of the Sundown Kid at the hands of Witchfinder Jones, I went a little crazy for awhile. I fled the carnage at Pilate's Basin and wandered the high plains for several days, in a feverish delirium. At times I thought Medicine Dog rode beside me, his blind eyes undaunted by the snow. Other times I fancied I saw Sundown standing on the horizon, waving me on. Other times I imagined I could hear Whatisit?'s moronic laughter echoing from the darkness.

On the third day out, poor, faithful Erebus literally dropped dead underneath me, spilling me back into reality. There was little I could do but eat the horse, which strengthened me enough to press on. From that moment on, I wandered the plains in my true-skin, preying on antelope, the occasional buffalo calf, and other four-legged creatures that crossed my path.

At the end of each day I would find an outcropping of rock or dig out an abandoned prairie dog burrow in order to shelter myself from the unceasing winds of the plains, and listen to the true wolves howling from the distant hill tops, like lost souls mourning their expulsion from hell. Sometimes I would take up the howl, only to hear confusion and mistrust in their reply. Even without seeing or scenting me, my wild cousins knew an unnatural thing when they heard it.

I wandered westward without planning it that way. I was leagues beyond my old tribe's hunting boundaries, moving towards lands undreamed of when I was a boy tending Eight Clouds' horses.

I have no way of knowing precisely how long I spent in the wilderness—at least two, perhaps three seasons, of that I'm certain. I steered clear of both Whites and Indians during that time. Since leaving the Comanche, I had found little joy in the White Man's world. And while I had known a certain friendship with the likes of Praetorius and Sundown, I knew their types to be few and far between. Buffalo Face and Medicine Dog were right—Whites were bad-crazy. Not all of them were as demented as Reverend Near, McCarthy and Witchfinder Jones, but it wasn't from a lack of trying. I had come to the decision that it was best not to trust Whites on general principles and give them as wide a berth as possible.

As for the Indians...well, I guess I didn't want to get close to anyone for fear of losing them. It seemed to me I was cursed. Everyone I had ever loved or befriended in my short life—for I was still shy of my twentieth year—had ended up killed. Some by my own hand.

My natural parents, who I never even got a chance to know, had been brutally taken from me when I was no more than a mewling pup. Then there was poor Flood Moon and Small Bear, whose deaths shame me to this day. After them came Praetorius and poor Whatisit?, left to feed the crows along some god-forsaken river bed. And now Sundown was gone, slain by the same murdering bastard that robbed me of my mother and father.

But there's only so long anyone—human or vargr—can spend alone before anger gives way to loneliness, which then sours into madness. I thought of McCarthy, isolated from the company of his own kind until his mind turned in on itself like a fox in a snare. I began to fear that I would lose control of myself and slip back into the red-eyed savagery that had cost me the woman I loved. I decided it was time for me to leave the wilderness and seek out others. Even if they weren't my own kind.

I smelled the wagon train before I saw it.

Its scent came to me on the wind, causing me to prick up more than my ears. For the wind smelled of female. Several of them. There was also the distant odor of smoke and something fainter, yet disturbingly familiar, that I could not place. Intrigued, I set out in search of what could produce such interesting smells.

Three miles later I crested a small butte and found myself looking down on a wagon train. It wasn't a big one, as such things went. There were four covered wagons, yoked to oxen, and a couple of horses and mules. One of the wagons had a busted wheel and the train was halted in order to fix it. From my vantage point, I could see a man dressed in the apron of a wheel-wright laboring beside the disabled wagon. He was large and fleshy, his head and face completely devoid of hair. I could almost see the sweat trickling down his smooth pate and dripping from his thin eyebrows.

But what truly caught my interest were the women—there had to be at least a dozen of them, all young and healthy. Some tended the cook-fire, others were mending clothes, while others simply stood around in groups and laughed amongst themselves, combing out their hair. Except for one or two, they were all obviously pregnant.

The sight of so many women made my groin ache. I did not know whether to be excited or disgusted. I had been with only one woman in my life, and that was Flood Moon. Part of me—the part I had come to think of as my *vargr* self—wanted to go down and do to the women what it had done to Flood Moon. The temptation to succumb to my wild self's desires was strong—but then I forced myself to remember Flood Moon's screams and how she had looked at me with hate in her eyes, and my ardor lessened. Still, I found myself scanning the encampment for signs of males apart from the wheel-wright.

A second man, just as chunky and bald as the first, emerged from the back of one of the covered wagons. He had a rifle in one hand, a knife stuck in his belt. None of the women paid him any attention. A third man, younger and not as heavy as the others, but equally hairless, rode up on one of the mules and dismounted beside the second man. The two bald men bent their heads over what looked like a map, looking up now and again to point in various directions.

My attention was drawn back to the females, and one in particular. She was younger than the others and one of the few not visibly pregnant. Her hair was long and unbound, hanging almost to her waist, and she had a habit of tossing her golden mane over her right shoulder, like it was a veil of spun gold. Perhaps it was her youth, or perhaps it was that I had gone so long without a woman, but in any case I fell in love with her in two heartbeats.

Whatever the case, the fact is that I was so bedazzled by this vision of loveliness, I did not realize I was being watched until my attacker was almost on me. Just before he struck, I got a strong whiff of the scent that had troubled me earlier. The familiar smell I could not place. I spun around, but it was too late. Something landed against the side of my head and all sound and vision fled. But not before I was finally able to recognize the strangely familiar odor.

It was the scent of my own kind.

The cold rag placed on my brow brought me back to my senses. As I started awake, the first thing my aching eyes happened on was an angel smiling down at me. My vision cleared and the angel turned into the beautiful young girl with the long blonde hair I had glimpsed tending the cook-fire.

I was trussed hand and foot and on the floor of one of the covered wagons. I was also in my human form and stark naked, to boot. I blushed despite myself. The girl giggled and drew her hand back from my brow.

"The intruder is awake, milord," she called.

"Excellent, Lisette," replied a male voice. "Leave us; I wish to question him alone."

As the girl vacated the wagon, the man who had spoken climbed in past her. Considering we were in the middle of wide-open nowhere, he was dressed rather extravagantly, sporting a single-breasted frock coat, dress trousers, an Inverness cape, and a beaver hat. With his long hair curled and brushed upward and parted in the middle, and his bushy mustache, he looked more like a dude on his way to the opera than a settler headed West.

The dude pulled a thinly rolled cigar the color of mud from inside his breast pocket and eyed me intently.

"What pack do you run with, cub?"

"Pack?"

The dude bit off the end of his cigar as fast and as clean as a guillotine, displaying strong white teeth. "Don't play stupid, cub. It won't work with me. Who is your Master of Hounds?"

"I don't know what the hell you're talking about, mister—"

He moved so fast I didn't see it coming. My head rocked back from the force of the blow to my jaw. I bared my teeth at the dude and growled as he moved to strike me again, which stayed his hand.

"My, aren't we the brave and loyal dog," he commented drily. "Well, don't show your fangs at *me*, little wolf—unless you mean business." With that, he thrust his face into mine. Before my eyes the dude's face flexed and twisted upon itself, as if something inside his head was trying to break free. His whiskers and muttonchops spread across his cheeks and chin as his nose grew longer and broader, transforming into a snout.

I cried out then, not in alarm, as one might suppose, but in surprise and delight. For I was finally face-to-face with that which I'd been seeking for the last five years—one of my own kind.

"You're like me!"

The dude dropped his wolf-face, resuming his human guise like a man adjusts his johnson on a hot day. "Of course I am, you wretched lout! What did you expect?"

"I—I wouldn't know, sir. I was raised by humans from an early age."

The dude fell silent, narrowing his eyes and fixing me with a strange look. He leaned forward, sniffing the air like a bloodhound trying to pick up a scent.

"You smell vaguely familiar. Perhaps your sire was known to me. Do you know his name?"

"No, sir. I was just a baby when my folks were killed."

The dude's eyes narrowed even further. "Killed? By humans?"

"Yes, sir. A bounty hunter who calls himself Witchfinder Jones."

At the mention of Jones' name the dude looked somewhat anxious. "Is that so? Would this `Witchfinder' be a large man? Very hairy?"

"Yes, sir. That's him!"

"I knew him from the Old Country, under another name. But it seems his occupation is still the same." The dude rubbed his chin and stared off into space for a long moment, then turned his gaze back on me. "You remind me of someone I once knew. His name was Howler. He came to this country almost two decades ago to try and start a new life for himself. He dreamt of founding his own pack, free of the squabbles and power-plays that plague the Old Country. No one has heard from him since. Perhaps he was your sire."

"What about my mama? Did you know her, too?"

"She was a human female, what else is there to know?" he shrugged dismissively. "If you are, indeed, what you say you are—a loner—I need not fear you. Come, let me show you some hospitality." The dude produced a knife from his breast pocket and freed me from my bonds.

"I am called Poilu, my young friend. And you are called—?"

I hesitated, uncertain which of my names was more suitable for the occasion. Since Poilu, despite his ability to shapeshift, was White, I decided to go with my White name. "Billy. Billy Skillet."

"How American. Here, allow me to have one of my wives find you some decent clothes. It wouldn't do to have you parading naked in front of the ladies."

Five minutes later I was dressed in a pair of linen trousers, a white dress shirt with too much starch in it, a loose-fitting sackcoat, and a pair of short Wellington boots. I hadn't been so finely tricked-out since my days as a drummer for Professor Praetorius. It had been so long since I had worn clothes that I had to fight the urge to revert to my true-skin and tear the garments to shreds.

"You look quite respectable, for an American," Poilu said, smiling slightly. "Come, allow me to introduce you to the rest of my entourage."

As I stepped from the back of the covered wagon, the first thing I noticed was that the afternoon had given way to early evening. The second thing I noticed was that the wagon train's company was seated around the central campfire, their faces turned towards us in silent anticipation.

A big, meaty man, bald and devoid of whiskers, got to his feet and approached Poilu, his eyes averted and head down. Although he no longer wore a leather apron, I recognized him as the wheel-wright. When he spoke, his voice was surprisingly high-pitched for a man so large.

"Milord, the wagon has been repaired, as you commanded. The train will be ready to move come the dawn."

"Excellent," Poilu smiled, displaying his magnificent teeth to full effect. "Billy, this is Henri, my major domo and master eunuch."

"Beg pardon?"

"Come now, my young friend. When one has a harem, one *must* have eunuchs."

I looked from Henri to the other two men—both of them hairless as well. There was no anger or resentment in their great, cow-like eyes.

Instead, they regarded Poilu with the reverence other hold for religious leaders or lovers.

"And here are my wives—" Poilu gestured to the eleven women clustered around the campfire. "Are they not beautiful?" Indeed, all of the assembled women were strikingly handsome. And, except for the blonde who had ministered to my wounds, every one of them looked to have a bun in the oven. They sat there, hands laced atop their swollen bellies like ancient fertility goddesses, imperturbable, impassive, and immutable.

"Evening, ladies."

"You needn't waste words on them, lad. I've had them all muted—except for little Lisette; the one who you spoke to earlier."

"Muted?"

"Yes—I had their tongues surgically removed. I find it keeps the bickering in the seraglio to a minimum. Besides, none of them spoke English to begin with. Except for Lisette. Her mother was British, her father Belgian. I allowed her to keep her tongue in order to have a human liaison capable of communicating with the peasants of this rough country."

"They're called settlers here, not peasants."

Poilu shrugged. "I can call a horse an equine and it still runs on four legs and produces manure. I must say, although you are of *vargr* blood, you do seem to have been infected with this country's mass delusion concerning democracy."

"I'm not used to thinking of myself as *vargr*. I don't know what the rules are, or how I'm expected to behave. You're the first one I've ever seen. Alive, at least."

Poilu fished another cigar from his tobacco case and bit the end off, spitting it into the fire. "There's no need to feel ashamed, Billy. Most *vargr* come into their power ignorant of what it really means. You see, *vargr* males outnumber females five to one. Unless a male joins a pack with a sexually active female, there's little chance of him breeding true.

And, once in the pack, you have to wait until the bitch queen is in season, and then you must fight all the other males for the privilege to rut. So, necessity decrees that he find breeding material elsewhere.

"Some take human females as life-mates, others propagate themselves through acts of rape, casting their seed upon the wind, as it were, while a few breed with true-wolves. In any case, most *vargr* born are of mixed parentage. Those sired by rape are the most plentiful. They are raised by humans, in the very bosom of human society, ignorant of their birthright. Many of these mixed-bloods are incapable of shapeshifting, although they possess the instincts and hunger of a *vargr*. These are the *esau*. Most of them are mad as march hares. The *esau* can be very dangerous indeed, and not just to humans."

Poilu reached inside his coat and produced a golden locket, flipping it open to reveal a cameo portrait of a woman, her hair piled atop her head in elaborate coils. "When I spoke of your sire earlier—and, the more I look at you, the more I believe that Howler was, indeed, your sire—I did not tell you the whole truth. Howler was my demi-brother. We shared paternity, not maternity. I was sired within the pack, he outside it. He often spoke to me of his dreams of coming to this country and starting afresh. He wanted to be the Alpha Prime. The Master of Hounds of his own pack." With a twist of his wrist, he snapped the locket shut. "Poor Howler. He always had such small dreams. As for myself—I am unwilling to settle for such a modest future."

"I don't understand—?"

"Come-come, lad! Why do you think I would travel to this god-forsaken country? For freedom? Liberty? No, I have come to build an empire! *My* empire!" Poilu gestured grandly at the land beyond the campfire's glow. "Howler was right—Europe is old and overcrowded. Asia even more so. If an ambitious *vargr* is to find his destiny, it will be here, in this great emptiness! There is nothing here to keep me from populating this vast expanse with my seed! Your father was satisfied to start with a single female—and look where it got him; an orphaned son ignorant of his birthright! But I have eleven wives, and soon I will have eleven sons—possibly even a daughter! And, in time, I shall breed with my daughters and granddaughters, and my sons with breed with their sisters, nieces, and daughters, and within two centuries all *vargr* that roam this land shall be of my breed. Or should I say our breed, nephew?"

Poilu did not wait for me to respond before barreling on. "You know the ways of this land, do you not? You are familiar with the human savages?"

"I was raised by the Comanche, if that answers your question."

Poilu clapped his hands, grinning broadly. "Excellent! Most excellent, indeed! I am in need of an experienced guide. While Henri and his *compeers* are loyal servants, they are far from expert when it comes to scouting. We have already lost one of the eunuchs to bad water. You will stay on and serve as our guide to the Territory of Utah." It sounded more like a command than a request. It probably was.

"Utah? Why the hell do you want to go there?"

"Because of the humans who call themselves `Mormons'. They practice polygamy as a rule, so a man with eleven wives would not call undue attention to himself in such a community."

"I reckon not."

"You will be our scout." Like I said, Poilu didn't ask people, he told them. Since I didn't see any reason not to go along with his plan—after all, I'd spent years in search of those such as myself—I decided to go along for the ride.

Besides, the whole time Poilu was going on about breeding a new race and sowing America's wilderness with his seed, Lisette had been giving me the eye.

I bedded down under one of the wagons, curling up on an old horse blanket I'd gotten from one of the eunuchs. I was tired and had a full belly and, truth to tell, it had been a busy day for me, so I fell asleep almost immediately.

I woke up later to the sound of hissing geese.

No. Not geese. Tongueless women.

While having their tongues removed might have reduced their bickering, as far as Poilu was concerned, it was evident his wives had devised a way of getting around their speech impediment. They sat around the dying campfire, hissing and gesticulating wildly. There was something ominous about the sight of so many heavily pregnant women discoursing amongst themselves in a private language. One of the eunuchs sat just outside their circle, a rifle cradled in his arms, but it was uncertain whether he was protecting the women from potential harm or guarding against escape. Finally the women tired of their strange conversation and returned to the wagons, followed by the gun-toting eunuch. I shrugged and went back to sleep, but my dreams were not easy.

Over the next few days, as I rode before the wagon train, scouting the territory that lay ahead, I reflected on my circumstance. After years of searching for those of my own kind, I had finally stumbled across not only a fellow shapeshifter, but a blood relation at that. Yet, there was a hollowness inside me. I always thought I would have been happier. Instead, all I felt was uneasiness.

Most of this I attributed to Poilu. I was glad my job allowed me to spend so much time away from his company. Despite our shared ancestry, I felt no kinship toward him. There was something disturbing about being around him, as if I was being smiled at by an enemy unwilling to show his true face. Yet, I was so ignorant of *vargr* custom and lore, I assumed my discomfort was born from a fear of seeming foolish in the eyes of my elder.

Whenever I returned to the wagon train, Poilu would debrief me and then, if I was lucky, talk about the Old Country. This soon became something of a ritual between us, complete with coffee served us by one of his tongueless wives. Poilu would treat himself to some cognac from a case he'd brought with him from Europe, along with his usual cigar. Realizing how little I knew of *vargr* etiquette and custom, he did his best to continue my ignorance, dispensing tiny dollops of information here and there to insure my continued willingness to serve him as scout.

Most of his stories began with him recounting something that had happened to him during his tenure as the Master of Hounds, the title given the consort to the Bitch Queen. To hear him tell the tale, he had been a powerful and much-admired figure. Then his beloved queen was killed, the victim of internecine warfare with a rival pack envious of her influence in the court of Napoleon III. Upon the death of the Bitch Queen, the center of the pack could not hold and they were forced to disband. Rather than swear fealty to those responsible for his beloved's murder, Poilu decided to leave the Old World in favor of the New.

Despite these chats, I did not find my uncle to my liking. Poilu was imperious and haughty, as cocksure as a Comanche brave who has never tasted defeat. And I was soon made well aware of how protective he was of his traveling harem. While I was in camp, the eunuchs never let their eyes wander from me for a moment. On more than one occasion I toyed with the idea of riding off and leaving the werewolf lord to whatever fate might await him, but the hope of learning more about myself—and the promise of a smile or kind word from the lovely Lisette—always reigned my horse back to camp.

Lisette.

Beautiful Lisette.

I can still see her face, smiling back at me through the years that separate us. She was so lovely; her skin smooth as a rose petal, her lips full and ripe as a peach. She smelled of cinnamon and cloves and woman. Her hair fell from her shoulders like a golden curtain, swaying in the breeze like a thing alive. She was beauty made flesh.

I knew it was foolish of me to fall in love with one of Poilu's wives. The older *vargr* made no effort to hide the fact that they were his property. Still, I was young and full of the juices all young males seem to overflow with. I found Lisette extremely attractive, and it was plain to see that she favored me as well. As I slept alone under the open skies, I found my self pondering whether Poilu would miss one measly wife. After all, we were kin. What harm could it do?

One night, after everyone had retired, I was awakened by the sound of someone approaching my bedroll. I sat up, shifting into my true-skin without conscious thought. To my surprise, I saw it was Lisette, dressed in a long white undergarment.

"What are you doing out here?" I whispered, sliding back into my human guise.

"I wanted to talk to you."

"Is that wise?" I glanced around warily, wondering where Poilu's prize castratis might be hiding.

"You needn't worry about the eunuchs. I put something in their coffee. They'll sleep for a hour or two."

"What about Poilu?"

She giggled and rolled her eyes. "I can handle him."

"I'm afraid I don't share your confidence. Please go back to the wagon, Lisette."

She smiled at me then, her child-bride innocence dissolving. "Why? Are you afraid of me, Billy?"

"I'm more afraid of what might happen if you stay."

She drew nearer, her hips swaying seductively with each step. She slowly opened the front of her undergarment, exposing the milky flesh underneath. I knew I should jump up and drag her back to her wagon, kicking and screaming if need be, but my body refused to listen to reason.

"I like you, Billy," she whispered as she knelt beside me. Her lips were so close to my face they grazed my ear. "You're young and hand-some. You're not old like him. You like me, too. I can see it in the way you look at me."

"S-sure I like you, Lisette. B-but—"

"You're scared of him."

"It's just that—"

"You needn't be scared of him, Billy. He's not as powerful as he makes himself out to be. If he really was, he'd still be in Europe. He was once the Master of Hounds, that much is true. But he was deposed by an younger rival. That's why he came here—so he wouldn't have to see the Bitch Queen with someone else."

"Who is this 'Bitch Queen', anyway?"

"Why, his mother, of course."

While I was digesting what she'd told me, Lisette took my hand and placed it atop one of her firm young breasts. My brain began to sput-ter like bacon in the pan, short-circuiting any attempts at rational thought.

"I want you, Billy. I want you for my mate. Take me, Billy—take me now."

I've always been an agreeable sort, so it didn't take much in the way of pleading to get me going. Within seconds we were rolling on the ground, all fear and common sense lost in a wash of hormones. I pushed Lisette's cotton shift up over her hips, exposing the moist hair between her legs, all the while fumbling with my own buttons. When I finally managed to free my johnson I discovered, to my dismay and embarrass-ment, the traitorous piece of meat was as limp as fresh wash.

"I-I'm dreadful sorry, Lisette," I blushed. "I don't know what's wrong. This has never happened to me before..." That part was true, since this was only the second time I'd ever been such a position with a woman.

Lisette grabbed me by my hair and pulled me down on top of her. She writhed against me like a hungry cat, her eyelids fluttering as if she was in the grip of a fever.

"While you're human you can't get hard. *Vargr* can only get it up when they're in their wild skins," she breathed into my ear.

She wanted me to change. She needed me to change. And the only way I could ever delve the sweet mystery between her legs was if I did change.

But I just couldn't bring myself to do it. Every time I closed my eyes to focus my attention on shifting from human to wolf, all I could see was Flood Moon's blood-smeared face, screaming in horror as I ravaged her.

I pulled away from Lisette, gasping like a man who has just narrowly escaped the pull of a whirlpool. My face was flushed and my eyes swam, but I was still wearing the skin of a man.

"I'm sorry, Lisette. I can't."

"What do you mean you can't? I told you how to do it," she pouted.

"I just can't. That's all there is to it," I muttered, turning away from her so she would not see the look of disgust and fear in my eyes.

Lisette's displeasure darkened her face, twisting her beautiful features into something far from pretty. "Poilu might be a wheezing old dog, but at least he knows what to do with a woman when he's got her under him!" she snapped.

If she was expecting me to respond to this goad, I'll never know. For there was a sudden, sharp report and her head, from the nose on up, disappeared in a spray of blood, hair, and bone. I was too stunned to do more than twitch when Lisette's brains splattered against my face and chest.

She sat there for a long moment after the top of her head disappeared, her hands still fluttering in her lap like wounded birds. Then her body slumped to the ground, as if it had suddenly become sleepy. I looked it the direction of the shot and saw Poilu standing by his private wagon. He looked tired and older than I'd ever seen him before. Even though the night was cool, he was dressed in a flannel night shirt and not his wolfskin. Beside him was one of the pet eunuchs, a smoking rifle gripped in pudgy hands.

"The little minx fancied she could poison me with her pathetic little herbal mixtures," Poilu snarled, his words somewhat slurred. "Thought she could cuckold me like I was no more than a miller or a barber-surgeon! Wretched little creature!" He stepped forward, whatever drug Lisette had put in his evening cognac slipping away as his skin became darker and hairier. "And as for you," he growled, lowering his head as his nose pushed and twisted its way into a snout, "you thankless little bastard, I'll deal with you like the dog you are!"

I shifted as the older werewolf came at me, leaping to meet his charge half-way. We struck head-long and began tearing at one another with all the fury of true wolves. He may have been old, but Poilu was far from weak and inexperienced when it came to hand-to-hand combat. But, then, I was far from a piker in that field, myself. Still, I'd never fought one of my own kind before, and I was unprepared for how strong my opponent was.

All my life I had been accustomed to creatures that were weaker than myself—and that included grown buffalo, mind you. But Poilu was powerful and knew where to bite and where to claw to do the most damage. While I had youth and vigor on my side, he definitely had years—if not centuries—of experience in dealing with rival *vargr*. Fur, blood, spittle, and shit flew in every direction as we rolled about on the ground. It wasn't until I felt a sudden heat across my shoulders and back, followed closely by intense pain, that I realized we had rolled into the campfire and set my pelt ablaze.

I howled in agony and snapped fiercely at Poilu, taking a couple of his fingers off as neatly as he would have bitten the ends off his cigars, but the old werewolf refused to let go.

"You were going to cuckold me, you worthless piece of shit!" he growled through bared teeth. "You were going to steal my Lisette from me and set up your own pack! Let's see how many cubs she'll bear you now, interloper!"

Poilu forced my head back, exposing the soft meat of my jugular, and for a moment it looked like I was truly done for. Although I had endured what would have been certain death for a normal human time and time again, I knew that a killing bite from one of my own would prove genuinely fatal. Just as Poilu lowered his head, there was a horrible, high-pitched scream from the direction of the wagons. Poilu, distracted, turned to see what was going on, and I used that moment to break free of his hold and put some room between us. I fully expected Poilu to press his attack, but to my surprise he seemed to have completely forgotten me.

The screaming continued. It was high and womanish—and for a second I thought it was one of Poilu's wives. I looked in the direction of the sound and saw Henri, Poilu's chief eunuch, standing as if transfixed, his chubby hands clutching his chest. There was blood coming out of his mouth. There was also an arrow sticking out between his red-stained fingers.

Suddenly the sky was full of burning arrows. They lofted upward then, like falling stars, plummeted to earth. Some of them thudded harmlessly to the ground. Most of them, however, landed in the canvas rigging of the covered wagons, setting them ablaze in seconds. Poilu's remaining wives poured from the burning wagons, their tongueless voices filling the night with mute screams.

Poilu stood on crooked legs and shook his fists at the night, bellowing at his unseen attackers like a vengeful Old Testament patriarch. "Who *dares*?!? Who dares attack Poilu!?!"

His only answer was a single rifle-shot, which caught him in the chest and hurled him backward a good ten feet. To my surprise, he stayed down, twitching like a dropped fawn.

I'd like to point out that I was hurt pretty good myself, by that point. I'd suffered some serious burns and sustained substantial internal injuries. I could feel myself bleeding inside and some ribs had snapped off and punctured my left lung. Poilu had also done a far amount of cosmetic damage as well, tearing off my right ear and biting through my nose so it bled like a sieve. Still, despite all that had happened, I crawled to where he lay dying.

"Poilu..?"

He was still alive, but just barely. Blood was pumping out of his shattered ribcage and running out the corner of his mouth. He looked stunned and more than a little shocked, like a child thrown from a beloved pony.

"Silver," Poilu whispered, his words made bubbly by the blood filling his lungs. "They've got silver bullets." And then he died.

I didn't need to hear any more to know who was behind the attack on the camp. I knew all too well. It was my very own private devil, come to make sure I didn't get lost on my way to hell.

Somehow—I'm not exactly sure myself, since I was rapidly becoming delirious from my injuries—I managed to drag myself away from the camp and escape into the night before Poilu's attackers swept down from their hiding place in the surrounding hills. I got as far as a rise overlooking the massacre before my strength deserted me entirely. Broken, burned, and bleeding from more than a dozen deep wounds, I looked on helplessly as more than twenty Whites—most of them sporting heavy beards—rounded up Poilu's harem. It slowly dawned on me that these were the Mormons Poilu had hoped to blend with and, eventually, prey off of.

The eunuchs were killed as they tried to protect their fallen master's wives. I'll give them one thing—they might not have had testicles, but those poor bastards certainly had guts. The women, unfortunately, did not fare as well as their keepers. Makeshift torture racks were made from the wheels of the unburnt wagons, and each wife was, in turn, stripped naked and lashed in place, her arms and legs spread wide.

It was then Witchfinder Jones stepped out of the crowd of gathered men. Even from such a distance, I had no trouble in identifying him, for he still wore my father's pelt as a shirt. I watched as he methodically gutted each of the pregnant females, yanking their unborn children out of their bellies and crushing them underneath his boot heel.

A great sadness filled me and I began to chant prayers to the Great God Coyote in the Comanche tongue. Somewhere along the fifth or sixth wife I blacked out, my eyes swimming with visions of half-formed things crushed to jelly and the screams of tongueless women ringing in my ears.

CHAPTER NINE

I don't know how long I was out. All I know is that when I came to, I was lying on a pony drag. I struggled to sit up, but the pain that filled my body made me stop. I fell back and moaned.

"You are awake, skinwalker?"

The voice made me open my eyes again, for it belonged to a woman and spoke in the tongue of the Shoshone, a cousin tribe of the Comanche.

The horse came to a halt and I heard the rider dismount and walk back to where I lay on the drag. Standing before me was a woman dressed in a long buckskin skirt and tunic, the front decorated with elaborate beadwork that marked her as a medicine squaw. She was neither beautiful or ugly, although I guessed her age to be no more than sixteen or seventeen. On her head was a cap made from the skull and pelt of a badger, its paws tied under her chin.

"Y-you are Shoshone?" I asked, my voice sounding so weak it frightened me to hear it.

She shook her head, causing the badger's empty paws to sway. "My mother was Shoshone, taken in a raid. My father is Lakota Sioux. Hunkpapa. I am called Digging Woman."

"Digging Woman—how did you come to find me?"

She smiled, and it was then I glimpsed the beauty and power held within her. "I saw you in a vision, Walking Wolf. I had traveled into the wilderness in quest of visions. The Great Coyote came to me and showed me where to find you."

I should have been surprised she knew my Indian name. But having learned at Medicine Dog's knee, I knew better. I had prayed to Coyote and he had heard my prayer, sending this woman to my aid.

I tried to sit up again, but the pain was still too great. Digging Woman's eyes flashed alarm and she pushed me back with a gentle shove.

"Do not try to move, skinwalker. Your wounds are grave. Give them time to heal."

As I scrutinized what little I could see of myself, I could tell she wasn't exaggerating. The backs of my hands and my forearms were covered with scar tissue—no doubt from the fire. I tried to touch my left ear—only to find a raw nub. My regenerative abilities were no doubt taxed to their limit. It would be some time before my body could rebuild itself properly.

"I owe you my life, Digging Woman."

She shrugged and pulled a handful of dried herbs from a pouch secured to her waist and handed me a drinking skin. "It is a long ride to my people's camp. Chew these and wash it down with water. It will help dull the pain."

I did as she said. Although I have a high pain threshold, something told me I'd be stepping over it quite a bit in the next few days. As with most unpleasantries, I was right as usual.

Digging Woman was a remarkable woman. If I did not have reason enough to consider her so from the start, I quickly came to respect my savior during the two days she dragged me through strange and, doubtless, hostile territory.

The Sioux were much like the Comanche, seeing how they were

both nomadic tribes that wandered the Great Plains and relied heavily on the buffalo for their day-to-day existence. Both tribes were noted for their ferocity in battle and skill as horsemen. Both were proud warrior societies. The big difference between the two, however, lay in their attitude toward religion.

Comanche, like I said earlier, were rather pragmatic people. They observed the taboos and rituals imposed by their gods, but did not put much stock in supernatural things. While medicine men were respected, they were not treated with the respect one gave war chiefs. The Sioux, on the other hand, were great believers in visions—and not just those given to shamans and elders. The Sioux went in for rituals and dances and saw signs and portents in many things.

Digging Woman was a wise woman, schooled in the knowledge of roots, herbs, grasses, and the phases of the moon. There was no such thing amongst the Comanche, unless you counted the Grandmothers who attended the women when it was their time to give birth. And, to judge by her dress and manner, Digging Woman had attained a great deal of stature within the tribe at an early age. Although the Sioux could be as dismissive of their women folk as the Comanche, the strength and truth of Digging Woman's visions and her skill as a healer had won her great respect from the various Lakota tribes.

She explained to me that she was born of a family famous for its medicine. Many great and powerful shamans had been born of her clan. In fact, her uncle was none other than *Tatanka Yotanka*, better known as Sitting Bull, the most revered of the Hunkpapa medicine men.

The night before we reached her tribe's camp, she informed me she would send a dream to her uncle, to tell him of their arrival. Later that evening, I saw what looked to be an owl rise from where she was sleeping, its muffled wings beating silently as it flew in the direction of her people. A coincidence? If I was a hundred percent White, and human to boot, perhaps I could believe that. But I have walked the thin line between the real and the unreal all my life, both as a Comanche brave and a shapeshifting werebeast, and I know better than to dismiss such things out of hand.

In any case, the very next day as we pulled into the Hunkpapas' camp, Sitting Bull strode from his *tipi* and warmly greeted his niece without anyone telling him we had arrived. I was able to understand most of what he said, as I'd spent the past couple of days learning as much of the Lakota tongue as possible. Once again my gift for languages had come in handy, allowing me to become fluent in a matter of weeks instead of months.

"Digging Woman! Little daughter! I saw you in a dream last night! It is good to know my vision was true."

"It is good to see you as well, uncle."

"In my dream, you said you were bringing back powerful medicine to help us in our war against the Whites. Is this true?"

Digging Woman hopped off her horse and gestured to me, wrapped in blankets and curled up on the pony drag like an ailing grandmother.

"Judge for yourself, uncle."

Sitting Bull frowned and moved to lift the blanket from my face. Groggy from the herbs used in blunting the pain that stitched its way through my body like lightning, I felt my nose elongate, become a snout, and I flashed my fangs in warning, lest he touch me. Sitting Bull's eyes widened and he stepped back from the pony drag, clearly shaken.

"Coyote!"

"Not Coyote. But one beloved of him. He calls himself Walking Wolf."

Sitting Bull nodded his head as he digested what she was telling him. "You have indeed done well, Digging Woman. Our medicine will indeed be made strong against the Whites! I will see to it that the skinwalker is made welcome."

That was my first meeting with Sitting Bull, and it would prove to be far from the last. True to his word, Sitting Bull had one of his subordinates surrender his *tipi*, where I spent the next month recovering from the grievous injuries dealt me by Poilu.

During most of that time Digging Woman tended to me personally, but Sitting Bull was often a visitor to my tent as well. There was much on the chief's mind, and he often talked with me when he was troubled. The Sitting Bull I knew then was still a young man, but he lacked the blood-thirsty brashness that marked so many of his fellow war chiefs. He was a thoughtful man, in his way. He reminded me of Medicine Dog, and I guess that was one reason I came to trust and respect him so quickly. When I looked into his eyes, I could tell he was a man who could see true.

Word soon got out that Sitting Bull was playing host to a skinwalker and many of the rival Sioux chiefs came to pay him homage. I distinctly remember the day Red Cloud, chief of the Oglala Sioux, rode into camp. Red Cloud was feared far and wide, by Whites and Indians alike. Before the Whites found their way onto the Great Plains, Red Cloud's name struck fear into the Utes, Crows, and Pawnees. A ruthless warrior, he was known as a man of pronounced cruelty, even by Indian standards. One story told how he pulled a drowning Ute out of the river by his hair, only to scalp the poor bastard once he got him to shore.

When he arrived at Sitting Bull's camp his party rode in whooping and shrieking, so everyone would know they were fierce and mighty warriors. Red Cloud was, by this time, an older man—older than Sitting Bull by a decade or more. He dismounted and Sitting Bull greeted him cordially. Red Cloud was a proud figure of a man, although he now limped from an imperfectly healed wound he'd received from a Pawnee arrow a few years back.

I was sitting in front of my *tipi*, wrapped in a buffalo robe and smoking my pipe. I had been amongst the Sioux the better part of a month and was close to being completely healed. My left ear had yet to grow back completely—I wasn't exactly sure why it was being so stubborn, perhaps because my attacker had been a *vargr*—but the burn tissue had all but disappeared, except for a thick patch on my right shoulder the size of an eagle dollar. I watched as Sitting Bull and Red Cloud strode in my direction. I could tell by the look in his eyes that Red Cloud was dismayed to see I wore the skin of a White.

"You told me you had a skinwalker, Sitting Bull," he protested. "How can this be a skinwalker when he is White?"

Sitting Bull simply smiled and said, "He is White on the outside, but hairy on the inside."

I lay aside my pipe and stood up, shrugging off my buffalo robe, and looked Red Cloud square in the face. It was a hard thing to do, for he indeed had the hard eyes of a born killer. And, without speaking a word, I shifted into my true-skin. Red Cloud's face showed no trace of fear or surprise, but I could see something change deep within those merciless eyes.

He nodded, more to himself than to show approval of me. "With such powerful medicine, we can not lose against our enemies."

He was wrong, of course. Horribly wrong. But at the time it seemed like the truth.

I spent thirteen years living as a member of Sitting Bull's tribe. They were good years, although far from idyllic. The Sioux were considered hostiles, since they didn't hold with the White government trying to build roads across their hunting grounds. Conflict was a constant part of Sioux life—as was death. But I had been raised amongst the Comanche, and the idea of being constantly at odds with those around you was far from unusual. Peace was good, but war was the way of things. This the Sioux and Comanche understood.

During those days amongst the Hunkpapa, I came to be regarded as a living good luck piece. Braves who wanted success on the war path came to me so I could bless their shields and arrows. War chiefs who needed help in keeping control of their braves came to me for support. Women heavy of child came to me, so I could breathe into their nostrils and impart the blessing of Coyote on their unborn.

In time I came to know all the great chiefs and warriors of the Sioux, not to mention the Cheyenne. They all came to my *tipi*, bringing gifts of ponies, food, buffalo robes, and fine beadwork. Their names read like a Who's Who of the American Indian; Rain-in-the-Face, Gall, Scarlet Point, Lean Bear, Black Kettle, Little Robe, Blue Horse, Dull Knife, Pawnee Killer, Little Thunder, Spotted Tail, Crazy Horse... All of them brave men. All of them now dead.

Soon I became quite wealthy, as the plains tribes judged such things, and I could take whatever woman I pleased to wife. So I picked Digging Woman. She might not have been a great beauty, but she was strong-minded, loyal, and fearless.

And what about my fear of shapeshifting during intimate moments, you ask? Was ours a marriage in name only? Certainly not. During my recovery, Digging Woman spent many nights underneath the buffalo robes with me, chasing the illness from my bones by pressing her body against mine. When my fever finally broke, my body celebrated its escape from death and I soon found myself atop Digging Woman, but she was not frightened by my bestial appearance and far from unwilling. For the first time in my twenty years of life, I found myself actually making love to a woman.

As Sitting Bull's nephew-in-law, my status in the tribe became even greater. The only thing that would bring even stronger good luck to the Hunkpapa would be if a child was born of the union between skinwalker and Sioux. And in 1868, I was presented with a son. No man could have been prouder or happier than I was on the day my first-born was presented to me, wrapped in the skin of a rabbit, squalling lustily and waving his tiny hands as if he would pull the clouds from the sky. His skin was covered with a light down, like that of a pup, and he yipped just like one when he was hungry. We named him Small Wolf.

As I held my son, I no longer wondered who or what I was. It did not matter if I was White or *vargr*, or even Sioux as opposed to Comanche. As of that moment I was one-hundred percent Indian. And I knew that from that day forward I would always be Walking Wolf, no matter what I might call myself in the years to come.

The seasons passed. Became years. The Whites eventually resolved their fight against themselves down South, and began refocusing their time and energies on winning the Indian territories. The government insisted on building a road to Bozeman along the Powder River, but Red Cloud would have none of it. He had threatened to fight all Whites who tried to use the Bozeman Trail, and constantly harassed the soldiers sent there to build the three guardian forts needed to secure the road.

Then, in December of 1866, just as the gray clouds hovering over the Bighorn Valley warned of coming snows, High-Back-Bone of the Miniconjous and Red Cloud conferred on how best to destroy the Whites stationed at Fort Phil Kearney, along the banks of Little Piney Creek. They came to me for my blessings, and I gave it to them, although I secretly feared their efforts would prove futile.

Red Cloud and High-Back-Bone marshalled their men and sent a small decoy party out to attack a wood train hauling timber to the post. A second decoy party, lead by Crazy Horse, rode boldly toward the front of the fort. Naturally, the commanding officer sent out his soldiers—eighty of them, to be exact, lead by a Captain William J. Fetterman. Crazy Horses's men fell back and Fetterman followed, over the high ridge to the north and down the other side, where close to two thousand Sioux and Cheyenne braves burst from hiding places along the slope. The startled, overconfident soldiers found themselves engulfed by a sea of arrows. None survived.

In what the Whites would call the Fetterman Massacre, the Plains Indians had succeeded in landing a solid blow against the Whites. With

Colonel Carrington and his remaining soldiers trapped inside their fort by the fierce winter weather, and the troops at Forts Reno and C.F. Smith equally incapacitated, Red Cloud and his companions had proven themselves to be more than ignorant savages, nipping at the heels of their betters.

To my private amazement, the government agreed to abandon the Bozeman Trail, confine military operations to defense of the existing Platte Road, and set aside eighty thousand square miles of the Missouri and Yellowstone river basins for exclusive occupancy by the Indians.

Now full of confidence, during the summer of '67 Red Cloud's war party attacked some wood-cutters near Fort Kearney, who barricaded themselves behind wagon boxes. As the soldiers were armed with the new breech-loading rifles, the war party was eventually driven off. However, the outcome at the Wagon Box Fight did not leave the Sioux feeling defeated. After all, they had denied the Bozeman Trail to all emigrant travel, trapped the soldiers in their forts, forced army supply trains to fight their way through, and had stolen enormous numbers of horses from the bluecoats.

When the government sent messengers into the hostile camps with an invitation of peace talks in Laramie, Red Cloud dismissed them out of hand. He was too busy preparing for the fall buffalo hunt to waste his time on such foolishness. As far as Red Cloud was concerned, he had won his war. But he had no way of knowing that the Whites had agreed to surrender the Bozeman Trail only because the Union Pacific Railroad was opening better routes to the Montana mines farther west.

The summer of 1868 was another good season for Red Cloud—he told the government's runners that he would not attend the Peace Commission's talks until Forts Phil Kearney and C.F. Smith were abandoned. And, at the end of July, he saw his demands carried out, as the soldiers marched out of Fort C.F. Smith, the northernmost post along the

Bighorn River. Flushed with victory, he rode down from the mountains and set fire to the abandoned encampment. A few days later he was able to do the same to the much-hated Fort Kearney, after its garrison left.

However, he still refused to attend the peace talks at Laramie. When I asked him about it, he said he would think about it after he had put in the winter's meat for the tribe. But by the time he finally got around to signing the Medicine Lodge treaty, as it was called, it had become a worthless piece of paper. Red Cloud had no way of knowing this, of course. The workings of White government was beyond him—he had no way of knowing that a new president had been elected. A president who had seen to it that the Peace Commission was permanently adjourned and had publicly announced that the settlers and emigrants headed westward were to be protected even if it meant the extermination of every Indian tribe. Like I said, there was no way he or any of the other chiefs who had put their names on the peace treaty could have known that.

But they would soon find out.

Black Kettle was a Cheyenne chief, much respected by his fellows, although he had lost control over some of his younger warriors in the last few years. Black Kettle was old and tired of fighting. He wanted peace with the Whites, and had been instrumental in talking many of the chiefs into signing the Medicine Lodge Treaty.

Angered when the bluecoats refused them rifles promised in the treaty, some of Black Kettle's more hot-headed young braves went on a raid into Kansas, killing settlers and stealing their horses. Their war party left a trail across the snowy prairies that pointed to Black Kettle's winter camp as starkly as a finger. On November 27, 1868, just as dawn broke, the blare of a military band woke the unsuspecting Cheyenne and brought them, sleepy-eyed, from their *tipis*. A bluecoat with golden hair ordered his men to open fire with their carbines. Black Kettle grabbed his wife and jumped onto a pony tethered outside his lodge and galloped for safety across the Washita River. A bullet struck Black Kettle in the back, while another struck his wife. They fell, dead, into the icy water of the Washita.

The Indian Wars had begun.

Over the next few years the White government's Peace Policy proved itself to be just words on paper. The tide of emigrants and settlers heading ever westward kept increasing. There was no end of the White Man and his covered wagons. The Sioux were not the only tribe to find their treaties violated—the Kiowa, Arapaho, Cheyenne, Comanche, and Apache all ended up lied to. Horses, blankets, guns and ammunition that had been promised them by the White Man's treaties in exchange for allowing trails to be build across their lands never materialized.

Equally disturbing was the effect the Union Pacific Railroad was having on the great buffalo herd that was the source of all life and social structure amongst the tribes that roamed the Great Plains. The railroad had, effectively, divided the buffalo into two herds, the northern and south-ern. At first the buffalo refused to acknowledge the iron horses that cut through their ancestral grazing ground, often blocking the tracks. Soon the railroad hired hunters, equipped with long rifles that could shoot as far as a mile away, to make sure the way was kept clear.

The Whites slaughtered the great buffalo in numbers undreamed of by even the mightiest Indian hunter. And, in what seemed to be genu-ine perversity on their part, the White hunters usually left the carcasses to rot where they fell, taking only a tongue or a hump in order to collect their bounty.

There was a madness on the land, and its name was Extinction.

In the spring of 1870, Red Cloud did what none had ever thought he would do. He rode to Fort Fetterman, Wyoming, named after the bluecoat he had helped kill four years before, and told the commandant that he wanted to go to Washington and talk to the Great Father about the

Fort Laramie Treaty and the possibility of going to a reservation. It is hard to say whether Red Cloud's desire for peace came from a need to protect his people from certain extermination or if he had simply grown weary of the war path. I do not know for sure, and I was there. In any case, Red Cloud never took up arms against the Whites for the rest of his life.

Still, he was far from a whipped dog. He had many complaints against the government, and he voiced them quite eloquently. The cold-blooded killer had, over the years, developed into a skilled statesman.

Red Cloud intended to trade and draw his treaty rations and annuities at or near Fort Laramie, although the government was equally determined to get the Sioux off the Platte and onto the reservation. Red Cloud gave in little by little, walking a narrow line between the White government and his own people. Any concessions not widely supported by the Sioux weakened his leadership—which rested, largely, on his ability to manipulate the Whites. Finally, in 1873, a compromise was reached. An agency would be created in northwestern Nebraska, just outside the boundary of the Great Sioux Reservation. The government built the Red Cloud Agency for the Oglalas and the Spotted Tail Agency for the Brules, their ancestral enemies.

Although the Whites saw this as a victory, it soon began to turn sour. Violence still proved a problem, contracting frauds plagued the agency from the very beginning, and the Sioux did not respond well to the Indian Bureau's high-handed attempts to "civilize" them by educating their children in the White Man's ways while stripping them of their language and culture.

Many of the Indians resented—or simply did not comprehend—the Whites' desire to keep them away from the settlements and travel routes. Indians off the reservation did not automatically mean hostility. They might be out hunting, or visiting friends and family in neighboring tribes, or just wandering around the country, seeing the sights. However, the Whites felt greatly threatened by the Indians' refusal to stay in one spot. The Indian Peace was as illusory as the treaties they had signed. Although Red Cloud stood fast, remaining on the reservation, hundreds of Oglala braves flocked to Sitting Bull and Crazy Horse.

The army, under the command of General Sherman, was determined to break the will of the free-roaming Indian tribes. They set forth to find the enemy in their winter camps, killing or driving them from their lodges, destroying their ponies, food, and shelter, and chasing them mercilessly across the frozen land until they died or surrendered. And if women and children were hurt and killed along the way—then so be it. And as the open land and the wild game that had once seemed inexhaustible began to disappear, the reservations began to be seen as the only alternative to complete obliteration.

Although Sitting Bull still held immense respect for Red Cloud, he considered him deluded. Reservation life was confining; the clothing and rations were often scanty and invariably of poor quality. The whiskey peddlers and other opportunists that were drawn to the agency were decidedly bad influences on the more impressionable young braves. As Sitting Bull once said at one of the tribal talks; "You are fools to make yourselves slaves to a piece of fat bacon, some hard tack, and a little sugar and coffee."

As it was, many of the Sioux traveled back and forth between the agencies and the nontreaty camps, enjoying the old hunting life during the spring and returning for the hardtack and coffee during the winter. The Indian Bureau saw these "unfriendlies" as dangerous, as they were ungovernable and sometimes raided along the Platte and the Montana settlements at the head of the Missouri and Yellowstone rivers. Still, as much as the Whites complained about the Sioux disregarding the treaty, they were busy breaking it in even bigger ways.

In 1873 surveyors laid out a route for the Northern Pacific Railroad along the northern margins of the unceded territory. And in 1874 "Long Hair" Custer, the hated murderer of Black Kettle, led his soldiers into the

Black Hills, part of the Great Sioux Reservation itself, and found gold. Naturally, miners swarmed into the territory and the government did nothing to stop them, except to make a lame attempt at offering to buy the land from the Sioux for a paltry sum.

It was at this time I had a vision.

I was asleep but in my dream my eyes were open and I could see someone was standing at the entrance of my *tipi*, watching me. When I looked harder, I saw the person watching me was none other than Medicine Dog. I was very glad to see my old teacher, but at the same time there was a strange feeling inside me.

"It is good to see you, Medicine Dog," I said, getting to my feet. "But are you not dead?"

Medicine Dog nodded and smiled. "Almost ten years, as the white man reckons time. Much has happened since I last saw you," he commented, pointing at Digging Woman and Small Wolf, still sound asleep on either side of me. As I drew closer to him, I realized that not only had he regained his vision, he now had both eyes.

"Why have you chosen this time to visit me, old friend?"

"I would give you a vision, Walking Wolf." Medicine Dog motioned for me to follow him as he held open the flap of my *tipi*. "One you would do well to heed." Without another word, the old medicine man slipped out of the tent. Uncertain of what to do, I followed him—and stepped out of Montana into the choking dust and heat of the Texas Panhandle.

I was more disoriented than frightened by the chaos around me. I had walked into the middle of a Comanche war camp, the braves painted for battle and preparing to meet their enemy. As I looked around, I recognized several faces, including those of Quanah Parker and Coyote Shit.

Everything seemed extremely real. I could smell the sweat of the braves, hear their war songs, even count the hairs on the tails of their pony—but no one seemed to be able to see either Medicine Dog or myself. Coyote Shit, who wore the buffalo headdress and sacred amulets of a medicine man, was busy evoking the blessings of the Great Spirit, but if he sensed our presence, he gave no sign.

As I looked about, I noticed that many of the assembled warriors were wearing strange-looking shirts decorated with eagle feathers and painted with symbols of power. As they listened to Coyote Shit's prophesy of victory, they became more and more agitated.

Medicine Dog did not try to hide his disgust as he listened to the man who had replaced him as the tribe's shaman. "The years have not served Coyote Shit well in wisdom. His vision is false. His medicine untrue. He has convinced these warriors that the only way for the Comanche to become a great nation again is to kill all the Whites they can. He has provided them with "medicine shirts" that he claims will turn aside the Whites' bullets." Medicine Dog spat, producing a sizable gob for a dead man. "They are doomed."

Before I could say anything, Medicine Dog grabbed my hand I felt myself shooting through the air like an arrow released from a bow. When he let go of my hand, I was standing on a distant hilltop overlooking the battlefield. I recognized the place as Adobe Walls, one of the oldest settlements in that part of the country. Below us, Quanah's warriors attempted to attack twenty-eight buffalo hunters barricaded in the ancient fort. The buffalo hunters were armed with rifles that could shoot a mile and bring down buffalo as easily as rabbits.

The first wave of Comanche rode in headlong, arms thrown wide, screeching their war cries, exposing themselves to enemy fire without fear. After all, they had their medicine shirts to protect them. Most of them were blown clear out of their saddles.

I shook my head and looked away from the slaughter below, only to find myself standing beside Coyote Shit. He was desperately singing prayers and working medicine, no doubt hoping to affect some change in his tribe's favor. A brave rode up from the battlefield, bearing a message from Quanah. Where was the magic promised them? Before Coyote Shit had a chance to respond, a stray bullet—fired by a rifle seven-eighths of a mile away—crashed into the hapless brave, splashing his blood all over the frightened medicine man. Not to mention myself.

Medicine Dog and I stood over Coyote Shit as he shivered and hugged himself, his eyes wide with fear. I expected Medicine Dog to gloat over his rival's downfall, but he looked sad, almost pitying.

"What will become of him?" I asked.

"Quanah will not kill him, if that's what you're thinking. He will forgive Coyote Shit what he has done. But he will not forget, either. Coyote Shit's power with the Comanche is at its end. He will turn himself in to the reservation with the others next year, and spend the rest of his days as an object of ridicule. He will live to be old. Much older than those who believed in his medicine shirts, at any rate."

"And Quanah?"

"He shall become old, as well. And fat. And corrupt. The reservation will make all of the great chiefs rot before their deaths."

"Why are you showing me these things, Medicine Dog?"

"So that you will see the folly that came to the friends of your youth, so that you might warn your adopted family of the trouble that is to come."

"But I don't understand—"

"Understand later. It is enough that you remember now." With that Medicine Dog touched my hand one more time, and I felt my body turn into lightning and shoot across the sky, back to the land of the Sioux.

When I opened my eyes again, I was back in my own *tipi*, my wife pressed against my side. As I puzzled what my dream meant, I lifted a hand to wipe the sleep from my eyes. The back of my hand was caked with the blood of a dead Comanche brave.

In the winter of 1875 runners appeared at the winter camps of all the nontreaty chiefs. They bore a grim message from the Great Father in Washington: they were to come to the agencies at once or be considered hostiles against whom the army was prepared to make war. Of course, Sitting Bull and the others chose to ignore the summons. As Sitting Bull was fond of saying, "the Great Spirit had made me an Indian, and not an agency Indian."

During the late winter months of '76, Digging Woman took Small Wolf with her to visit her sister, who was in a village on the Powder River. I was loathe to let them go, but Digging Woman had not seen her sister in a long time, and the aunt was a particular favorite of our son. On March 17th of that year, General Crook led an attack on the village. It was a short but vicious skirmish, and did more than its share of damage against my family. While Digging Woman managed to escape unharmed, her sister was shot while attempting to flee. Eight-year-old Small Wolf, standing over his fallen aunt with nothing but a toy spear for protection, was shot through the head by one of the bluecoats. There was little pleasure to be taken from the knowledge that Crook had bungled the follow-up to the attack and was forced to retreat in the face of winter.

When the news reached me of my son's death, I was inconsolable. After all I had endured to live the life of a normal man, one who could look forward to his son growing up and taking his place beside me, it was nearly enough to shatter my spirit. Our son—our only child—was dead at the hand of the Whites. I screamed and howled like a thing gone mad and ran into the snow covered hills on all fours, baying at the frigid moon until my lungs bled. Digging Woman was equally distraught. She cut off her braids and burned them as a token of her grief, ritually cutting her breasts until they were wet with blood. Sitting Bull assured us both that there would soon come a time for vengeance against the bluecoats. And that it would be sweet indeed.

By June of 1876 the number of Indians fleeing the reservations for the nontreaty camps had reached epidemic proportions. There were twelve hundred lodges represented, and easily two thousand warriors gathered in one place. Our camp along the Greasy Grass River extended for three miles. Never had there been such a gathering of tribes in the history of the Plains Indians. Hunkapapa, Oglala, Brule, Miniconjou, Sans Arc, Blackfoot, Northern Cheyyene—they were all there. Several powerful and influential chiefs made camp with Sitting Bull, among them Black Moon, Hump, Dirty Moccasins, and Crazy Horse. None of these men were looking for a fight, but neither would they avoid one, should it come looking for them.

Earlier that season we had staged the annual Sun Dance on the banks of the Rosebud, where Sitting Bull had received a vision of great strength and clarity. He claimed to have seen many dead soldiers fall into our camp as if they were dolls dropped by fleeing children. Everyone liked this vision and no one doubted its truth, for Sitting Bull was known to be a true-seer. And, besides, he had the luck of Coyote at his right hand—how could his medicine not be strong?

Then news came that bluecoats were marching down the Rosebud. Crazy Horse took a large war party and rode off to do battle. They fought the bluecoats for six hours, after which Crazy Horse called off the fight and the soldiers retreated. While this fight had been good, Sitting Bull knew it was not the battle he'd seen in his vision.

Meanwhile, General Terry was approaching from the east, Colonel Gibbon from the west. They joined on the Yellowstone at the mouth of the Rosebud, and Terry sent out a strike force of six hundred calvary under the command of Custer. The same Yellow Hair Custer who had violated the sanctity of the Black Hills, the most holy of Sioux places. Custer followed the Indian trail up the Rosebud, across the Wolf Mountains, and down to the Greasy Grass, which the Whites called Little Big-horn.

I did not take part in the Battle of Little Big Horn. Neither did

Sitting Bull, for that matter. Shortly before Custer's regiment arrived on the scene, we retired to the nearby mountains to work our medicine. We were so wrapped up in our prayers and rituals, we did not hear the clash of sabers and the crack of gunfire until the battle was well underway.

I remember looking down at the blue-clad figures scurrying about in the dust. The smell of their fear rose to greet me on the wind. Most time fear smells rank and animal, like sex. But the fear that day smelled sickly sweet, like dead roses, for they knew they were going to die. As I watched my adopted people slay those responsible, in part, for the death of my son, I knew I should feel elation or victory. Instead, there was a taste of ashes in my mouth.

I turned to Sitting Bull and said; "The Whites will not let this go. They will hunt us down like wild animals."

Sitting Bull shrugged. Although he could not read or write, he was far from a fool. He knew that bringing down a White war chief was a dangerous thing to do. "Better to be hunted down like wolves than to live like dogs."

After the battle was over and the gunsmoke had cleared, we left the mountains and headed into the valley to count the dead and aid the wounded. Over the years all sorts of wild tales have come out of Custer's Last Stand. The one that gets repeated the most is that Crazy Horse took Custer's scalp for his lodgepole. That's pure bull-crap. The other story is that Sitting Bull cut open Custer's ribcage and ate his heart. That's an out-and-out lie. I was there and I can testify that Custer's body was not mutilated in any way. We *did* butt-fuck the bastard, but that's a different thing entirely.

What should have been the Plains Indians' greatest triumph ended up being their undoing. Custer's massacre shocked and outraged the Whites and it shook the Peace Policy to the point of collapse. It also brought a flood of bluecoats into Indian country, and rationalized the forcing of agency chiefs into selling the Black Hills to the United States.

Within a few days of their victory at Greasy Grass, the various bands broke up and went on their way. Some even headed back to the reservation. Despite being faced with a common enemy, it was still difficult to get the different tribes to band together. Little Bighorn was an exception, not the norm. Tribal rivalries and intertribal animosities remained as strong as ever. Although tribes would occasionally band together against the Whites, it would never last for long. The individual character of tribal society kept those capable of bringing together diverse opinions and philosophies from gaining any power. Although Sitting Bull was greatly respected, he could not hold a three-mile-wide camp together. Then again, the Indians did not see war as the clashing of armies, but the maneuvering of war parties. And that is where they were doomed to fail.

Man for man, there wasn't an Indian brave who couldn't lick his weight in bluecoats. But braves, no matter how skilled in the ways of war, were not soldiers. And faced with the discipline and organization of the U.S. Army, there was no way they could compete. Hell, they hadn't even invented the damn wheel yet.

Five months after Custer's Last Stand, eleven hundred cavalry under the command of Colonel MacKenzie fell on the villages belonging to Dull Knife and Little Wolf, hidden in a canyon of the Bighorn Mountains. Forty Cheyenne were killed and the rest were forced to watch the soldiers burn their *tipis*, their clothing, and winter food supply. The temperature plunged to thirty below that night and eleven babies froze to death at their mothers' breasts. Those who managed to escape made their way to Crazy Horse's encampment on the Tongue river, but the soldiers followed them there as well.

On May 6th, 1877, not even a year after the death of Custer, Crazy Horse led his Oglalas into Red Cloud Agency and threw his weapons on the ground in token surrender. Four months later he was dead, stabbed by a soldier's bayonet during a skirmish with guards.

Sitting Bull, on the other hand, refused to surrender. Rather than go to the reservation, he led his people northward to Canada. The army watched the boundary line like a hawk the whole time, making sure Sitting Bull didn't ride into Montana to hunt buffalo.

While the Hunkapapas got along with the redcoats, there simply was not enough game available to feed them. After four increasingly lean years in Canada, Sitting Bull finally surrendered to the United States government at Fort Buford, Montana. However, Digging Woman and I were not in the group that rode onto the reservation that summer day in 1881.

I figured that if the Whites had trouble with Indians like Sitting Bull and Crazy Horse, then they certainly would make life difficult for one such as myself. So I took my wife and disappeared into the wilderness, preferring the life of a renegade to that of a reservation squaw man.

CHAPTER TEN

After Sitting Bull surrendered and went on the reservation, I took my wife and built myself a camp on Paintrock Creek, up in the Big Horn Mountains. While the White government was adamant about keeping Indians on the reservation, they tended to turn a blind eye to settlers who'd set up housekeeping with squaws. And, to the casual observer, that's all I was.

Digging Woman suffered more than I did from being separated from her tribe. The Sioux, like the Comanche, were a social bunch, given to getting up and visiting one another whenever the mood struck them. It didn't sit well that she should be kept from seeing her various sisters, aunts, and other kinfolk.

When, miracle of miracles, she came up pregnant again, her hankering to visit her folks became so strong there was nothing I could do but let her go. A lone squaw traveling back and forth wouldn't have raised suspicions, but I was still fearful she would be caught and forced to stay on the reservation for good. But my fears proved to be unfounded. Digging Woman managed to sneak in and out of the Pine Ridge Agency, where Sitting Bull's people had been placed, without anyone being the wiser. In fact, she became so adept at it over the years, I stopped worrying about her trips altogether.

However, the stories she brought back concerning the quality of life on the reservation were troublesome enough. The reservations might have seemed ideal for the Whites, but they were proving extremely unhealthy for the Indians corralled upon them. Where once crime had been rare within the tribes, and most disputes were settled by giving ponies to the aggrieved parties, now the White agents dealt harsh punishments to even the most trivial offender. There were few pleasures allowed them, as the native dances had been banned by the authorities and the missionaries were busy stamping out many of the ancient customs that had held the tribes together for centuries.

A communal, nomadic people by nature, they were suddenly expected to appreciate and respect the value of individual land tenure and free enterprise. And, to top it all off, they were expected to dry farm in flinty badlands soil that wouldn't have raised a prayer.

Their rations consisted mostly of cheap green coffee beans, coarse brown sugar, and wormy flour. Half-wild longhorns were occasionally turned loose to be hunted on horse-back by braves desperate to reclaim a fraction of the pride given them by the buffalo hunts of old. Those chiefs and elders who had not been bribed into embracing the White Man's ways with gifts of sewing machines, oil lamps and iron bedsteads spent much of their time dreaming of the old days, when the buffalo were dark upon the land and the White Man a minor inconvenience.

Bereft of leadership and stripped of their traditions, the younger members of the tribe began to succumb to the apathy that had consumed many of their elders. The Sioux and Cheyenne women began sleeping with soldiers for food. The young men, desperate for adventure but denied the traditional war path, began enlisting as Army scouts or Indian Police, even if it meant being pitted against their own people. More and more Indians were taking up "citizen's dress", wearing the shabby castoffs provided by the missionaries instead of the traditional breechcloth and blanket.

The proud Sioux who had brought the mighty Custer low had been cruelly broken by the Whites. While I grieved for my friends, I could see no way of freeing them from the fate destiny had delivered.

In 1884 I was given a second child—another son. Like his brother before him, he was born with a pelt of light fur that fell away within a week of his arrival, leaving him hairless everywhere except his legs, for some reason. So we called him Wolf Legs. He was a good natured child; bright and inquisitive and with the brave heart of a true warrior. He was my pride and joy, and when I held him in my arms the day of his birth, the love I felt for him was almost enough to make me forget the loss of my firstborn son. Almost.

I was a happy man in those days. When I look back on that time, I see it through an autumnal haze, as if the nine years I spent along Paintrock Creek was one long Indian Summer. I was living free, away from the misery of the reservations. I had a sod lodge, divided into two areas, one for eating, the other for sleeping. Although my camp was far from the agencies, many of the southwestern tribes and sub-tribes sought me out over the years. Most came seeking visions from the fabled Walking Wolf, Hand of Coyote, or cures from his shaman-wife. Some of them could still afford ponies, blankets, pemmican, and beadwork in exchange for my services, as in the old days, but most were too poor to give me anything besides their respect.

Even though the fortunes of the tribes had dwindled, the number of braves seeking help did not slack off. Somehow these young men always managed to find their way to my camp, most of them rail-thin and wracked with fever by the time they arrived. Many died on my doorstep. I have no way of knowing the number who died along the route.

1889 was a very bad year for the Sioux. During that summer the beef herds issued to the Indians were decimated by anthrax, and a terrible drought and grasshopper plague destroyed what few crops they had. And, to top it all off, nine million acres of their best cattle range was stolen from them by way of a convoluted government boondoggle. About this time the pilgrims to my camp began to speak of a phenomena amongst the reservation Indians that made my ears twitch. There was talk of a strange new religious movement sweeping the tribes. Something called the Ghost Dance.

I questioned a Sioux warrior named Young Mule about it. Although he had made his way into our camp as close to death as any man could be and still draw breath, when he spoke of the dance his eyes took on the fiery gleam of a fanatic.

"The Ghost Dance was dreamed by Wovoka of the Paiute. In the dream he saw a time soon coming where the Whites will be swept from the land. The earth will be reborn and those family and friends the Whites have sent to the Spirit World will be returned whole. The buffalo will return in their numbers and we will be free to hunt and follow the herds as in the days of the Grandmother Land."

"That's a very fine vision, Young Mule. How does this Wovoka plan to make it true?"

"We are to dance the Ghost Dance. If enough of us dance long enough, and if we please the Great Spirit, then the believers shall be suspended in mid-air as a flood of new soil engulfs the earth, swallowing the Whites whole. Wovoka has promised this shall come in three years' time. Wovoka has also promised that he will take away the Whites' secret of making gunpowder when the time comes for the Renewal, and any gunpowder the Whites might still possess will be unusable."

I tried to listen as politely and noncommittally as possible, but I didn't like the sound of it at all. For one thing, for a religion designed to rid the Indians of Whites, it sure smacked of the White Man's belief. It especially reminded me of the Mormons, who I had held in contempt since the night they attacked Poilu's camp and helped slaughter his wives. It did not make me feel any better to know the Ghost Dance had spread throughout the territories and had been embraced by many tribes, including the Ute, Mohave, Shoshone, Cheyenne, and Kiowas.

Deeply disturbed by what Young Mule had told me, I decided it was time to venture onto the reservation and speak to Sitting Bull face-to-face and see where this nonsense was going. So I saddled up a pony and kissed my wife and son and rode out in the direction of Sitting Bull's camp, forty miles southwest of Fort Yates.

When I arrived, I got to see first hand the depredations done to the Sioux by the reservation. The abject poverty of the tribe was shocking. While they had lived free they possessed none of the things that Whites consider "wealth"—they had no gold, or precious gems, or houses full of furniture—but they had possessed the wealth of their world; buffalo robes to keep them warm in the winter, meat to keep their families fed, ponies to ride, beads to work into their ceremonial costumes. Now they were stripped of even the most meager pleasures of their former lives, reduced to beggars panhandling crumbs and cast-offs from their jailers. Still, there were still those who clung to their pride, refusing to bow completely to the dictates of the White Man.

One such man was Sitting Bull.

As I rode into Sitting Bull's camp, dozens of eyes watched me. Since I was wearing the buckskins of a mountain man, most did not recognize me as Walking Wolf, but assumed I was just another agency employee, sent by McLaughlin, the head of Pine Ridge's Indian Bureau, to keep an eye on the troublesome old chief. As word of my arrival spread, Sitting Bull left his two-room cabin to see who the intruder might be.

Although I had not laid eyes on the Hunkpapa medicine man in eight years, there was no mistaking him. He was bow-legged, like most Indians, from his years on horseback and now walked with a pronounced limp, from an old wound he received on the warpath, years ago. His thinning hair was carefully oiled and plaited, and his massive jaw and piercing eyes made him look like a great bird of prey. In defiance of the agency, he wore the traditional fringed shirt, leggings, and moccasins of smoke-tanned buckskins, a trade-cloth blanket draped around his waist. As he drew closer, his thin lips pulled back into a warm smile, showing fewer teeth than I remembered.

"I dreamt last night that a wolf walked into my camp and smoked the peace pipe with me before the fire. Now here you are, old friend! Welcome to my camp, Walking Wolf!"

At the mention of my name the Indians who had been looking daggers at me began to talk excitedly amongst themselves. I got off my horse and hugged the old man.

"You look as young as the day we worked our war medicine on Long Hair Custer," he laughed. It wasn't really a joke. I had stopped aging—at least noticeably—somewhere about my thirtieth birthday. As it was, at forty-three Digging Woman looked old enough to be my aunt instead of my wife. "Come, sit with me before the fire and smoke tobacco. There is much we must speak of, Hand-of-Coyote."

Sitting Bull's "lodge" was an exceptionally humble two-room cabin he shared with his three wives, his son, Crowfoot, and one of his nephews, a deaf-mute boy named John. It smelled of grease and smoke and sweat. As I we sat before the small cook-fire, Sitting Bull pulled out a small bag of government-issue tobacco and placed it in his ceremonial pipe.

"Why have you come to see me, old friend?" he asked quietly, lifting an ember to the pipe's bowl.

"I would ask you about the Ghost Dance."

Sitting Bull grunted and handed the lit pipe to me. "Kicking Bear brought the Ghost Dance back with him after visiting his cousin, Spoonhunter, in Wyoming."

"Kicking Bear? You mean old Big Foot's nephew? He was always something of a hothead, if I remember correctly. Hardly the kind to turn prophet."

Sitting Bull nodded, as if I was saying things he himself believed but dared not speak aloud. "This Ghost Dance is a strange thing. I have seen it performed. There is power in the dance, that I can not deny. But I am not certain the visions it gives are true.

"While I do not trust it, I do not forbid it. Kicking Bear's voice is powerful. Almost as powerful as mine. His disciple, Short Bull, is as dedicated as he is—and even more headstrong. If this Ghost Dance makes my people happy and gives them something to believe in—even if it is a thing that will never be, then where is the harm?"

"What of the Whites? How do they feel about the Ghost Dance?"

"It worries them. To know that my people dance for their destruction—it makes the Whites sweat, even though they do not believe it will come to pass."

"What about McLaughlin?"

At the mention of the Pine Ridge Agency's chief bureaucrat, Sitting Bull spat in disgust, making the meager fire sizzle. "McLaughlin would have my scalp, if his chiefs in Washington would permit it. He would have all Sioux sing from the missionaries' books and chop off our braids. He knows I am against that and he fears me."

"Perhaps he's jealous of you. I'm sure he'll never have the chance to perform before the Queen of England."

Sitting Bull smiled and straightened up a little bit. "Yes. The Great Mother. Those were good days, when I rode with Bill Cody. Not as good as when we killed Custer, but better than now."

There was a knock on the door and one of Sitting Bull's wives answered it. Short Bull entered and approached Sitting Bull. "Greetings, father," he said. Sitting Bull was not Short Bull's father, but all Sioux used the honorific when addressing their chiefs and respected elders. "I bring word from Kicking Bear. He would hold the Ghost Dance tomorrow in honor of Walking Wolf's arrival in our camp."

Sitting Bull lifted an eyebrow and looked at me. "Would you be interested in witnessing the dance, Walking Wolf?"

"Of course. But why tomorrow night? Why not hold it tonight?"

Short Bull looked somewhat surprised that I was unschooled in the ritual of the dance. Having grown up Comanche, I still harbored a mistrust of the Sioux's obsession with mystic rigmarole.

"The leaders and dancers must fast for a full day before entering the sweat lodges for purification."

"Oh. Of course."

"Tomorrow then," Sitting Bull agreed, ending the audience. After Short Bull was gone the old medicine man shook his head. "They will try and use you to give credence to the Ghost Dance."

"I know. But I still want to see it for myself."

Just before dusk the next day, I went with a hundred others from Sitting Bull's camp to a site a few miles away, where sweat lodges had been built. The men and women crawled into separate lodges. I had not undergone the sweating ceremony in several years, and I had forgotten how the heat opened the pores and allowed the toxins trapped inside the skin to pour out. It was like purging yourself of everything holding you to the material plane. At the end of the ceremony the dancers crawled from the lodges, where they were painted red by medicine men and their bodies were rubbed down with handfuls of sweet grass.

As I watched the others dress themselves in their finest regalia, a young Sioux medicine man called Black Elk handed me a carefully folded bundle.

"You honor us with your presence, Walking Wolf. It would give me great pleasure if you wore this shirt I made."

"Thank you, Black Elk." I held up the garment and studied it. It was a shirt of unbleached muslin, cut like the old-time ceremonial war shirts, with fringe on the sleeves and seams, but marked with strange symbols and with eagle feathers tied to it here and there. I felt there was something horribly familiar about the shirt as I put it on, but I could not pinpoint the source of my ill-ease.

The dancers, male and female, young and old, seated themselves in a huge circle around a dead tree with colored streamers tied to its branches. Kicking Bear, the official leader of the dance, sat at the base of the tree. At his command, a young girl came forward and was handed an elk-horn bow and four arrows made with bone heads. As we watched, the maiden dipped the arrows in a bowl of steer's blood and shot them into the air, sending one to each of the four points of the compass. Then the bow was tied to the branches of the tree and the maiden took up the sacred redstone pipe and held it to the west.

The dancers began to chant, their voices joining in a plaintive drone as Kicking Bear passed around a vessel of sacred meat. The dancers got to their feet as one and joined hands, shuffling slowly. I had been raised Comanche, where the sexes were strictly segregated during any public observance, and the sight of men and women dancing together was indeed shocking.

The dancers continued chanting and dancing, their eyes shut as they worked to conjure forth the image of a world free of Whites. A world where the buffalo ran unhindered. A world where all those slain by the White Man came back from the Spirit World, whole and untouched. During the next few hours the weaker members of the dance collapsed, one-by-one. Exhausted but exhilarated, their eyes burning with renewed hope, they spoke of having glimpsed dead loved-ones and friends.

"I saw Walks Backward, who died at Black Kettle's camp."

"I saw Blue Drum, who died at Dull Knife's camp."

"I saw Queen-of-Flowers, who was raped and shot by settlers."

And so on and so on.

After the fourth hour, many of the dancers had collapsed and were recovering on the sidelines, watching the heartiest and most fanatical of their number continue the dance. Suddenly, Black Elk broke away and snatched up a rifle and, to my surprise, leveled it right at my chest.

"The Great Spirit has given to me a vision!" he crowed. "A vision of power! All who dance the ghost dance—all who wear the ghost shirts—shall be made invulnerable! The White Man's bullets will turn from us and be no more than the stinging of insects!" And with that, he shot me.

The bullet kicked me onto my back, but even as I fell I remembered why Black Elk's shirt had seemed so familiar. Over the years I had all but forgotten my dream of Coyote Shit and his "bullet-proof" medicine shirts, but now that it was too late, it was coming back to me. I could hear Medicine Dog's voice echoing in my head;

See the folly that befell the friends of your youth. So that you might warn your adopted people of that trouble that is to come.

But it was too late. The damage had been done.

The assembled ghost dancers were gasping and pointing at me in amazement. Blood stained my ghost shirt a bright crimson as I got to my feet. I knew that whatever dark path the Sioux would find themselves on in the future, there was no way I could hope to steer them from it.

I glowered at Black Elk and Kicking Bear, but said nothing. Both men no doubt had heard Sitting Bull's stories of my apparent immortality. I had known from the outset they would try to make it look as though I supported the Ghost Dance, but I had not guessed at their ambition. I had been outside the tribe too long. I'd forgotten how ruthless medicine men could be when in search of power.

I staggered away from the dance site, brusquely shoving away those who wanted to touch the blood stain spreading across my chest. Although I was in pain and greatly angered, I did not allow myself to shapeshift in front of them. It was bad enough that Kicking Bear and his disciples had used me to validate their Ghost Shirts, but I refused to allow them to say Coyote had made himself manifest to bless the Ghost Dance.

I left for home that very same night. As far as I was concerned the Ghost Dance was nothing more that a con job being run by unscrupulous petty chiefs, willing to manipulate their peoples' desire to return to a simpler time to their own benefit. If ever there was proof that the White Man's madness had finally rubbed off on the Indians, this was it.

I spent the next several months doing my best to ignore the growing phenomena of the Ghost Dance. It was especially aggravating to discover that many of my old friends—men and women whose opinions I had once valued—had embraced the movement. I guess I should count myself lucky that Digging Woman was not taken in by it.

If 1889 had been a bad year for the Indians, 1890 was certainly heaping insult atop injury. With the "savages" penned up on reservations and the countryside supposedly made safe to settlers, immigrants literally streamed into South Dakota, most of them Scandinavians and Germans who went by the description of "honyockers", a good number of them by bringing scarlet fever and the grippe with them.

During the spring the Indian office ordered a new cut in the beef issue, which was already scanty to begin with. And, if the tide of active Indian resentment against the Whites wasn't high enough already, although Congress adjourned for summer without passing Sioux appropriations or making sure that emergency funding was available, they somehow managed to find the time to make a law prohibiting the killing of wild game on the reservations.

The bureaucrats stationed at the agencies might have not been the most honest or intelligent of men, but with so much anger, resentment, and bitterness building up on the reservation, it didn't take a genius to figure out that something was bound to blow. And the most visible sign of discontent were the Ghost Dancers. The heads of the Pine Ridge, Rosebud, and Lame Deer Agencies put their heads together and decided it was about time they tried to defuse the situation.

In late August one of the senior bureaucrats at the Pine Ridge agency rode out to No Water's camp to confront him about the Ghost Dance. No

Water refused to hear the agent out, and when he attempted to have the old chief arrested, he suddenly found himself faced with three hundred armed Ghost Dancers. Needless to say, his report to Washington did not sit well with his superiors.

A couple of weeks later Young Mule—the very same Sioux who had struggled to make his way to my camp the year before—and his companion, Head Swift, killed a settler. Two days later, they rode into the Lame Deer Agency and attacked the troops stationed there. It was a foolhardy gesture, of course, as there were at least seventy men to their two. Both died wearing their Ghost Shirts.

In October McLaughlin tried to order Sitting Bull to come to the agency for questioning concerning the Ghost Dance. Although the true leader of the cult amongst the Sioux was Kicking Bear, the Whites insisted on believing Sitting Bull was behind it all, simply because the old medicine man refused to denounce it. Needless to say, Sitting Bull ignored McLaughlin's orders.

In early November the Brules, under the direction of Kicking Bear's disciple, Short Bull, deserted their homes and followed their leader to Pass Creek, which marked the boundary between the Rosebud and Pine Ridge agencies. Although this upset the Whites a great deal—no doubt they had visions of marauding Indians in their heads—you have to bear in mind, up until this point, despite their warlike behavior, the Ghost Dancers still intended to hold out until they were joined in this world by their ghost relatives. As far as they were concerned, there would be no need to fight the Whites. But the agents in charge of running the reservation were hardly in touch with the Indian way of thinking.

The government, already nervous over the reports of the mysterious "Indian cult", ordered all whites and mixed blood agency employees in the reservation's outlying camps to abandon their schools, farms, and missions and come into the agency for protection. It also instructed all the Indians considered "friendlies" to gather on White Clay Creek.

A few days after Short Bull's exodus, two hundred Ghost Dancers swarmed the Pine Ridge agency, virtually taking over all the offices and buildings, hurling files and requisitions into the street and trampling them underfoot.

Five days later, the Sioux found themselves shorted yet again on their beef cattle rations. A Ghost Dancer began haranguing the crowd, soon inciting them to near-riot. The only thing that kept violence from breaking out was the intervention of Jack Red Cloud, old Chief Red Cloud's son. Two days after that, soldiers sent from Fort Robinson in response to McLaughlin's telegraphed plea for assistance marched into Pine Ridge. It just so happened to be the Seventh Cavalry—Custer's old unit.

The sight of their old enemy's former regiment sparked a panic amongst the assembled Indians, friendlies and hostiles alike. Convinced they were being set up for Custer's death, they piled their pony drags with *tipis* and winter clothes and moved west of Pass Creek, to join the Ghost Dancers already there. Once there, Short Bull and Kicking Bear decided their numbers had swollen to such numbers that they needed a new camp, one where they could feel secure against possible attack by the bluecoats. They picked The Stronghold, a two hundred foot butte known to the Whites as Cuny's Table. It would be impossible for anything to sneak up on them there without being seen.

However, while on their way to the Stronghold, many of Short Bull's Brules—who tended to be somewhat high-spirited even in the old days— got their blood up and attacked a settlement of squaw men and mixed bloods at the mouth of Porcupine Creek. Ranches and homes were wrecked, horses stolen, harnesses and wagons chopped to pieces, cattle driven off and, to top it all off, they burned the government beef ranch to the ground.

Of course, I had no way of knowing this at the time. I had a few visitors who made a point to keep me current as to the state of the tribe, most of them mixed bloods who were allowed to travel freely between the agencies. But where I kept my camp was a good three or four days ride from the Pine Ridge and Rosebud agencies, so by the time I heard what was happening on the reservation, it was usually old news. But sometimes I had visitors who came to me in dreams.

Just after Thanksgiving I woke from a particularly troublesome dream to find Sitting Bull seated, cross-legged, beside my cabin's hearth. He was smoking his peace pipe and looking fairly calm and composed. At first I imagined that my wife's uncle had somehow succeeded in smuggling himself out of Pine Ridge and had come to us for sanctuary. Then I realized that the medicine man was as substantial as the smoke rising from his pipe. Only then did I know that I was dreaming.

"Uncle! Why do you come dreamwalking?"

Sitting Bull looked at me with surprise in his eyes. "This is a dream?" Heaving a weary sigh, he turned into smoke and disappeared up the chimney.

I found the dream confusing, and thinking it was probably not an authentic visitation, dismissed it out of hand. Then the next day Digging Woman said; "I had a strange dream last night. I dreamt that my uncle came to visit us, then turned into smoke and went up the chimney. What do you think it means, husband?"

I lied and told her it probably meant nothing—that it was a silly dream, nothing more.

A week later I awoke once more, this time to find an Indian I did not know sitting in front of the fire in the same place Sitting Bull had occupied.

"Who are you?" I asked warily.

The strange Indian turned to look at me and smiled. Although his face was younger than I had ever seen it, his hair as dark as a raven's wing, I recognized my old mentor, Medicine Dog.

"Do you not know me, Walking Wolf?"

"Grandfather!" I gasped. "You are younger than I ever knew you in life!"

The dead medicine man nodded. "It is the way of the Spirit World. The dead grow younger here, walking back through time, from elder to brave to boy. In time I will be so young I will not be born—then it will be my time to return to the land of the living, dressed in the flesh of a new life."

"Does this happen to all the dead—or just Comanche?"

"There are many spirits here, gathered in great herds like the buffalo. Many are from places strange to me when I was alive. It is most interesting. Eight Clouds Rising, your adopted father, is now no older than the son that sleeps by your side. He will be reborn as a temple dancer in someplace called Siam. Longhair Custer is here, too. He is to be reborn as a sled-dog in a place called Alaska."

"But why are you in my dreams, grandfather?"

"I am here to warn you."

"Of what?"

"I am not certain."

"Grandfather—does this have anything to do with the Ghost Dance?"

"In its way. The ritual you call the Ghost Dance is not what its disciples think it is. No dance, no matter how sacred, can ever hope to pull the dead back into the world of the living. We shall return, but only in the way I described to you. This dance, however, is more than capable of pulling the living into the land of the dead."

"Grandfather—what are you telling me?"

"The Ghost Dance has set a series of events in motion. Blood—rivers of blood—will be spilled in the next few days. But perhaps it can be averted if one thing is kept from happening."

"What is this thing?"

"The murder of Sitting Bull by his own people."

"Then it will never come to pass. No Sioux in their right mind would dare to raise a hand against Sitting Bull!"

Medicine Dog shook his head sadly. "The wheels are already in motion. The one called McLaughlin is awaiting word from his chiefs so he may have Sitting Bull arrested. Once he has approval, he will call his Indian Police to him and order them to Sitting Bull's camp."

"But what do you expect me to do—?"

Medicine Dog held up a hand for silence. He seemed to waver before my eyes like the reflection in a troubled pool. "I came to warn you— I spoke of the danger to your friends, but I have not finished. There is a darkness coming your way, Walking Wolf. A darkness familiar to you, yet still a stranger. Be wary, Walking Wolf, for the darkness would eat your soul."

"Grandfather, what is this darkness you speak of—?"

"My time here is over. I can say no more. Farewell, Walking Wolf." Medicine Dog's body was now as thin as a cloud on a hot summer's day, and with a wave of his hands, he disappeared into himself.

I'm not proud of the fact I lied to Digging Woman the day I left. I told her I needed to go off on a vision quest. That I needed to be alone in the wilderness for a few days in order to commune with the Great Spirit. I knew if I told her I was on my way to try to prevent the murder of her uncle, she would have insisted on coming with me, and I feared that she and Wolf Legs would either be hurt or taken from me. It was not an irrational fear. I knew that if McLaughlin was desperate enough to go after Sitting Bull, anything might happen.

Still, ours was a special marriage, and it pained me to be deceitful—even when I had her best interests at heart. I do not know if she completely believed me—she had her own inner sight and spirit-visions, not all of which I was privy to. She was not happy with my leaving, considering the first of the punishing winter storms would soon strike the camp. I remember looking back at her and Wolf Legs standing in front of our cabin, watching me head into the mountains. They looked so small—almost like dolls. I lifted a hand in farewell and, after a moment, Digging Woman and Wolf Legs waved in return. For a moment I was overwhelmed with a surge of love for my wife and son that was so strong, so profound, it knocked the wind out of me. I came close to turning my pony around and heading back to camp right then, but for some reason I didn't.

I told myself I'd make it up to my wife and son when I got back. Of course, I had no way of knowing that was the last I would see them alive.

It gets cold in the Dakotas early on and hangs on like a pup to the teat. By the time I saddled up and headed for Sitting Bull's camp most folks, Indian and White, had already settled in for the season, barricading themselves against the heavy snow storms and brutal sub-zero tempera-ture. But the winter of 1890 was far from normal, especially for the Sioux. Still, I was astonished, on my second day out, to run across a band of Indians traversing the hostile winterscape.

The band's leader was none other than Big Foot, an elderly chief once respected for his wisdom but whose people had fallen on exception-ally hard times. There were close to a hundred of them, shivering and starving as they trudged through the snow. I could tell with a glance that most of them had the fever. Big Foot, wrapped in a trade cloth blanket that was no replacement for the buffalo robes of old, seemed glad to see me. Although it was close to zero, he was sweating and his eyes burned.

"Greetings, Big Foot. Why are you away from your winter camp?"

"Have you not heard? Custer's old regiment has been brought in to punish the Sioux once and for all. They would wipe us out so we can not perform the Ghost Dance one last time!"

"You're headed for the Stronghold?"

"My nephew, Kicking Bear, is there. He has promised not to start the last dance until I have joined him."

I looked at the rail-thin, fever-stricken men, women and children who comprised the band of pilgrims. Most clutched spears and stone axes, while fewer than a handful carried firearms. Even a blind man could see they were far from the warpath. "Big Foot, if you continue on your way, many of your number will perish."

"It does not matter. Come the dance, all shall be returned from the Spirit World."

I knew there was no point in arguing the point with the old man, so I rode on, leaving them to whatever fate they had dealt themselves.

It was December 15th when I made Sitting Bull's camp, the dim winter sun climbing toward noon. The sound of female voices raised in mourning struck me between the ribs as surely as an arrow. I had come too late.

A couple of crude huts still smoldered, and in front of Sitting Bull's lodge lay the bodies of several men, placed side-by-side, shoulder-to-shoulder. The women of the camp huddled near by, rocking back and forth and weeping. Some of the women had cut off their braids and tossed them, like empty snake skins, at the feet of their slaughtered men folk, while others rent their garments and slashed their bared breasts with knives and sharp rocks.

As I lowered myself from my horse, I realized I knew all of the dead men. I recognized, Catch-the-Bear, Brave Thunder, Black Bird, and Spotted Horn, all warriors I had fought alongside and hunted with during my years with the Sioux. One brave's face had been so savagely kicked in there was no way of identifying him—it wasn't until later that I discovered that it was Crowfoot, Sitting Bull's eldest son. But, to my relief, I did not see the medicine man's corpse on the ground.

I spotted an old Indian I had been friendly with in the days before Greasy Grass hovering at the edge of the mourning, his face so grief-stricken it seemed at first to lack all expression, and went over to speak to him.

"Strikes-the-Kettle, my old friend, what has happened here? Where is Sitting Bull?"

Strikes-the-Kettle shook his head, passing a hand before his face as if to block some horrible image from his mind's eye. "Sitting Bull is dead."

"Dead? How?"

"Yesterday Shave Head of the Metal Breasts came to the camp to speak with Sitting Bull. Sitting Bull allowed him to share his lodge for the night. Then, just before dawn, Shave Head opened the door to the lodge for his friend Bullhead and the others. They had been hiding across the river the whole time, drinking whisky to make them brave. They had bluecoats with them. They had come to arrest Sitting Bull.

"Bullhead grabbed Sitting Bull and dragged him outside. But they were so noisy, everyone was awake and coming out of their lodges, angry that the Metal Breasts would try and do this thing to our chief. Catch-the-Bear pointed his rifle at Bullhead and told him to let go of Sitting Bull. Bullhead just laughed, so Catch-the-Bear shot him in the leg. Bullhead shot Sitting Bull in the left side as he fell down. Then Red Tomahawk shot Sitting Bull in the back. So I shot Shave Head and then shot Bull-head twice.

"In all the confusion Tall Bull, Sitting Bull's horse—the one he was given by Cody—broke loose and sat back on its haunches and raised one hoof in salute. The Metal Breasts became scared then, thinking Sitting Bull's spirit was in the horse. That was when the bluecoats took charge, firing into the crowd, killing Catch-the-Bear, Black Bird, and the others.

"Bullhead was bad hurt—dying—but he ordered the troopers to

shoot Crowfoot in revenge. Red Tomahawk kicked Crowfoot's face in, then started hitting Sitting Bull's head with a neck yoke. The bluecoats and the Metal Breasts went crazy then, ransacking the camp and burning the lodges of those who dared stand against them.

"When they were finished, they loaded Sitting Bull's body onto a wagon, along with the bodies of the Metal Breasts. They said they were taking Sitting Bull back to the agency for burial."

"What of the *wotawe*, Sitting Bull's war medicine?" I asked, fearful that one of the drunken Indian police or troopers might have taken my old friend's most sacred personal possession as a trophy.

"It is safe," Strikes-the-Kettle assured me. "John, Sitting Bull's deaf-mute son, smuggled it out of the camp. That much we have been able to save."

"Strikes-the-Kettle, did they say *what* they were arresting Sitting Bull for?"

The old warrior shook his head, tears running down his seamed face. "Does it matter?"

By rights, I should have turned my horse around and headed back home. I had failed in my mission—reaching my destination almost six hours too late. But, instead, I rode in the direction of the Pine Ridge agency—a collection of trading posts, schools, and office buildings clustered behind garrison walls.

The troopers guarding the entrance to the agency looked at me funny, but because I appeared white, they let me in. The first thing I saw was Sitting Bull's corpse, propped up in a crudely-fashioned pine box in front of the blacksmith's. There was quite a crowd gathered there, composed mostly of the settlers who'd been called into the agency for protection against the "savages", and I had to shoulder my way to the front to get a look at my old friend's remains.

Sitting Bull's head had been reduced to a pulp, the jaw twisted so that it was positioned under his left ear. I counted at least seven bullet holes in his body. A sign was hung around his neck which read: *Sitting Bull: Killer of Custer & Enemy To All Americans.*

Tears of rage burned the back of my throat and I had to turn away to keep from losing control of myself. It would have been so easy—and so sweet—to simply cast aside my human skin and fall upon the killers of my friend. But I knew there was nothing to be gained from such an action—unless it was my death. I had yet to die from a gun shot wound, but I wasn't sure if having an entire garrison emptied into my hide might not prove fatal.

One of the armed guards standing watch over Sitting Bull's pitiful remains was a member of the Indian Police—those who Strikes-the-Kettle had called 'Metal Breasts'. To my surprise, I recognized him as High Eagle, a Sioux warrior who had once followed Sitting Bull in the days before the surrender. The older Indian recognized me as well and shifted about uneasily, trying not to meet my eyes, but I would not let him get away so easily.

"So, High Eagle," I said in the tongue of the Lakota. "Are you proud of the thing you have done today?"

High Eagle stiffened at my words and met my gaze. What I saw in his eyes spoke was sad and horribly aware. "We have killed our chief. What is there to be proud of?"

I did not bother to look at Sitting Bull's body again. I got on my horse and rode back out of the agency. What else was there for me to do but go home? I had no way of knowing that once word of Sitting Bull's assassination reached the Ghost Dancers that Kicking Bear would saddle up for war. Nor could I have known that in ten days' time Big Foot's band of starving, pneumonia-ridden pilgrims would meet their final, futile end on the banks of the Wounded Knee Creek. In any case, it would not have changed what I found when I got back to my own camp, several days later. At least, I like to tell myself that.

CHAPTER ELEVEN

It was colder than a politician's heart that winter. I'm not just talking about the amount of snowfall—which was sizable—but the harshness of the weather. As I rode across the Wyoming grasslands, where the buffalo had once roamed as thick as fleas on a hound's ear only a handful of years ago, an ice storm came whipping down out of the mountains. The ice froze to me almost immediately, and I was forced to shift into my true-skin to keep from freezing to the saddle. As it was, my pony wasn't faring well. I was forced to find shelter and wait out the ice storm, huddled against my mount for warmth.

That night my dreams were full of Sitting Bull's ruined face and the sound of women wailing. But amidst my troubled slumbers, I thought I could hear a familiar voice calling my name. The voice was distant and feeble, as if the person was trying to yell over the howling of the winter storm. I struggled to identify the voice. And then, with a surge of fear, I realized who it was that was calling my name. It was Digging Woman.

I started awake, terror racing inside my gut like a live mouse. Something was wrong. Something was horribly, horribly wrong. My horse was close to dead, but I somehow got it to its feet and forced it on its way. Not much later it died, collapsing into the snow without so much as a whinny.

Although foot-sore and frozen, I kept plowing on through the bitter cold, possessed by a desperate need to reach my wife and child that transcended all rational thought.

I finally reached camp on Christmas Day. The snows had relented and the pale winter sun shone down on the place I had called "home" for almost to a decade. Even from a distance I could tell there was nothing left alive.

The humble two-room cabin my wife and I had first made, then raised, our son in was nothing but charcoal and snow-flecked soot. Although the barn was left standing, the corral was full of dead horses, all shot through the head.

I found what was left of my wife and child not far from the ruins of the house. I did not see them at first because they were covered with snow. I tried to cradle Digging Woman's body in my arms, but she was frozen to the ground.

Digging Woman was missing her eyes, tongue, nose, breasts and scalp. Wolf Legs was relatively untouched, except that he'd been skinned from knees to ankles. As if their mutilations were not humiliation enough, their attacker had pissed in their wounds.

I dug through the charred remains of my home until I located a kettle and took the axe from the barn and chopped a hole in the creek, so I could draw water. I then built a fire and boiled the water and poured it over the bodies of my wife and child, although it still required my inhuman strength to pull them free of the cold, hard ground they had died on. Still, it was impossible to move their limbs into anything resembling repose.

The Sioux—like most Indians—believed that what physical indignity done to a dead body would be carried by that person into the Spirit World. The only way to right such a disgrace was cremation. I could not bear the idea of my poor Digging Woman and Wolf Legs going into the afterlife bearing such grievous injuries, but finding the fuel to build a suitable fire was impossible. The best I could do was to stash them in the hayloft of the barn and, where the animals would not be able to get to them until after the thaw.

As I tended to my dead family, my face made rigid by a sheet of frozen tears, I did not have to ask myself who could have done such a cruel and heartless thing. I knew who was responsible for the death of my wife and child, even though I had no evidence to prove it. I'd known the identity of the culprit from the moment I woke with my wife's dying screams ringing in my inner ear. Their slayer was the one who had, forty-six years earlier, slaughtered my parents and left me an orphan; the same butcher who, twenty-nine years ago, killed my best friend. The destroyer of all I had ever loved and held dear to me wore the face of a man, but was a demon in disguise. A demon sent from the very bowels of hell to make my life miserable. And the demon's name was Witchfinder Jones.

It wasn't hard for me to figure out where my quarry was headed. Even though he must have known I'd follow him, he made no effort to hide his tracks. He was moving high into the Bighorns, where the snows would be even heavier and the cold even more extreme. No one in their right mind would have dared set out under those conditions, into such hostile terrain, with close to no food, no horse, and unarmed. But I wasn't in my right mind—I was crazy. Crazy with grief. Crazy with hate. Crazy with guilt. All I could think of was how my wife and child must have suffered under that bastard's knife, and how I would find peace only after I'd torn the life from his body the same way he'd tortured my wife; slow, mean and evil.

I cut strips of meat from the horses he'd butchered, knowing in advance I was not apt to find much in the way of game so late in the season. I did not know if I could starve to death, but I was unwilling to weaken myself. I wanted my strength up when the time came for me to send Witchfinder Jones back to hell.

He had at least a two day head start, and he was on horseback, but

I did not let this discourage me. I had stalked Apache as a barefoot boy, tracked renegade Pawnee as a Sioux brave; I was not about to let a blizzard keep me from finding the man responsible for the murder of my family.

I struggled along the snow-choked mountain passes for more than three days, trying my best to ignore the frigid winds that bit into my flesh like a whipsaw. During that time my mind closed inward and began feeding on itself. I could see Witchfinder Jones, unchanged from our last meeting, grinning maliciously as he gouged Digging Woman's eyes from her head with his silver buck-knife. But part of me knew that couldn't be right. It had been almost thirty years since I'd last run across Jones. And, assuming he'd been a young man when he disposed of my parents, he'd have to be well into his sixties by now. Granted, Jones had been an impressive physical specimen, considering he'd lived through having his skull cracked open like a walnut, but he was only human, after all. But, surely, my dreaded personal demon was an old man by now.

I did not know what I had done to attract this human monster's ill-will, but he had been the bane of my existence from almost its very beginning; he was the bloody-handed architect who had set my feet on the strange and twisting path I had walked since the day Eight Clouds Rising found a squalling baby hidden inside a frontier smokehouse. By killing my natural parents, Jones robbed me of self-knowledge and my heritage as a *vargr*, and now, by slaughtering my family, he had squashed what chances I had of being a loving husband and doting father. Without my family to give me purpose and to make me whole, he had reduced me to the level of a beast.

Very well, if he wanted to turn me into an animal, I would be happy to oblige. Stripped of mercy, hope and love, I stalked my prey through the mountain wilderness, with no thought in mind save to taste my enemy's blood.

I spotted the cabin on the fourth day out. I knew I was getting close when I found Jones' horse—frozen stiffer than a missionary's dick—the day before.

I knew the cabin to be the property of a mountain man who went by the name Clubfoot Charley. I'd traded with him a few times over the years, and found him a decent sort, if given to the eccentricity common to Whites living alone in the wilderness. There was a thin plume of smoke rising from the chimney, and I hoped Charley had chosen to ride the winter out in one of his cabins on the lower slope, instead of staying put to mind his traps. There was no point in sneaking' up on the cabin. I was expected.

I opened the door without knocking. The heat from the pot-bellied stove struck me like a invisible hand, making my frost-bitten ears feel as if I was wearing red-hot coals for earmuffs. The smell of cooking stew wafted from a bubbling pot atop the stove. Seated at a crude table next to the stove were two men. Both were big and burly and sported beards, but there was no mistaking Witchfinder Jones.

Although I knew he had to be well into his sixties, there was only the lightest hint of silver in his heavy beard and long, matted hair. A large, puckered scar ran along his left brow. It looked as if someone had roughly shoved the split halves of his skull together and saddle-stitched them shut. His left eye was white as an egg, the pupil gone cloudy, but outside of that, he was little changed from the first time I saw him, twenty-nine years ago. He was even dressed the same, even down to the wolfskin shirt that had once been my father.

"Howdy, Billy," Jones said. "Long time, no see. You'll have to pardon my dinner companion," he gestured with his spoon. Clubfoot Charley was stripped naked to the waist, his head thrown back, mouth and eyes wide open. If that didn't tell me he was dead, the gaping hole in his chest sure did. Most of his right breast had been carved away, revealing the ribs beneath.

"He wasn't one for the social graces, even when alive. Beside, you've got me at a disadvantage, brother," Jones smiled, spooning a mouthful of stew into his maw. "I'm in the middle of dinner."

Despite all the hours I'd spent fantasizing what I'd do to my enemy once I caught up with Witchfinder Jones, I found myself at something of a loss. I had expected to find Charley dead, but I certainly hadn't reckoned on Jones eating him.

"You look confused, Billy," Jones chuckled. "Close the door and pull up a seat, brother."

"I no longer call myself Billy. And I'm not your brother, murderer."

"Oh, but you *are*, Billy. We're as much kin as Cain and Abel. Or haven't you figured that out yet?"

Jones seemed intent on distracting me, toying with me. But I was determined to have none of it.

"I've come to kill you, you murdererin' filth, for what you done to my family!"

Witchfinder smiled a slow, nasty smile that made me want to rip it off his face. "Which family would that be, Billy? The squaw and her half-breed cub, or the werewolf settler and his human bitch?"

"You know me, then?"

"Aye, I knew you from the moment I laid eyes on you in McCarthy's cabin, all those years ago. Just as you knew your sire's pelt and your dame's teat. Blood knows blood, brother. There's no denying it."

"Stop callin' me brother! I ain't your brother!" I snarled, bringing my fist down hard on the table. Coarse grayish-silver hair sprouted across the backs of my hands and up my arms as my teeth grew longer. "You killed my brother over forty years ago!"

"That boy wasn't your brother," Jones said, his voice completely serious. "He was a servant Howler brought over from the Old Country. In a year or two he would have undergone the induction ceremony and been ritually castrated, like all human males must be if they are to serve the pack. Remember Poilu's brace of eunuchs?

"I guess you want to know why I've done all this; why I skinned your sire? Why I torched your home and killed your wife and child? It was on account of a blood feud. Because of what your sire did to my mother—and to me." Jones leaned back in his chair and stroked the wolf-shirt like he would a pet, fixing me with his good eye. "How old do you think I am?"

"I don't know—sixty-five, perhaps. Although you don't look no older than forty."

"I'll be eighty-seven come next July."

"That's bull shit!"

Jones smiled again, and this time when he spoke, he allowed the accent I had first heard in his voice, years ago, to come to the fore. "It started in a country called Rumania. My mother was a beautiful young woman of gypsy blood. Her people had long known, feared, and, in some cases, served the wolf-lords and bitch-queens of the *vargr*. When a handsome and influential *vargr* noble decided to take her as a brood mare, she chose to look upon it as an honor, not a disgrace.

"For the first few years, our family was happy enough. My sire kept us in high style, in an isolated chateau, with servants to wait on us hand and foot. I did not see him much, as he spent most of his time at the Bitch Queen's floating courts in Paris and Vienna. But, during the brief periods when he was at home, he was a proud, if somewhat aloof, figure I worshipped from afar. Then, on my twelfth birthday, my sire took me to Paris, where I was presented to the Bitch Queen.

"She was indeed a *grand dame*, dressed in lace and expensive silks, her hair fixed with ribbons and smelling of perfume. She looked the same age as my mother, even though I knew she was older than the kingdoms of Europe. I was so intimidated by her high manner, I could do no more than tremble. As my sire pushed me forward, her eyes widened and she sniffed the air about me like a hound scenting a blooded animal. The smile on her face faded and grew cold.

"She turned to my sire and said; 'You have not bred true, Howler. The whelp is *esau*.'

"I never forgot the look my sire gave me that day. The pride and hope that had been in his eyes a moment before was suddenly gone, replaced by a loathing that stung as surely as if he'd swatted me with a bundle of nettles. It was as if I had done something so terrible, so disgusting, that it had curdled what love he ever had for me. And I had no idea what it was that I had done to earn my sire's hatred.

"I had been judged *esau*. Although sired by a *vargr*, the human blood in me was too strong. While I might possess the instincts, the needs, and the hunger of a true-born *vargr*, I would never shapeshift. Because of that, I could never be one of the pack. No matter what I did, I would never be accepted as *vargr*. And, as such, I was useless to my sire. I was imperfect—a genetic freak—a mongrel of the worst sort.

"My sire no longer had any use for me or my mother, who had yet to produce any more live issue, although she'd endured several painful pregnancies and miscarriages over the years. My sire turned us out of the chateau that had been my home since my earliest memory with nothing more than the clothes on our backs.

"My mother, no longer young, and made unattractive by her failed pregnancies, tried to go back to her people, but they would have nothing to do with her, as she had willingly consorted with an unholy thing. They were especially hostile to me, since I bore the Mark of the Beast." Jones gestured to his thick eyebrows and hairy palms.

"My mother was never a strong woman, and the years spent pampered did not prepare her for such cruelty. Cast aside by my sire and shunned by her own people, it was not long before my mother lost her mind completely.

"She began to believe that she was, indeed, the devil's mistress and began threatening the local villagers, demanding tribute in the form of food or money, or she would put the Evil Eye on them. It worked, at first. But, in her madness, she eventually went too far with her demands and the townspeople stopped being frightened and began to get angry. A year after my sire turned us out, she was accused of being a witch and hanged at the crossroads of a village in Translyvania. I would have died with her as well, but I somehow managed to escape the mob.

"It was then I decided to vent my rage on the unnatural world. To become a witchfinder-for-hire, if you will. Vampires, werewolves, and ghouls held no horror for one such as myself. I might be incapable of shapeshifting, but I am a *vargr* born." He rapped his chest with a clenched fist. "I was raised savoring the taste of human flesh. I was taught to see humans as cattle to be herded and culled. And then, after all that, he cast me aside—hurled me in with the cattle and ignored my pleas for help and guidance!

"The blood of the wolf-lords runs strong in my veins. I do not age like mortal men—or even other *esau*. And I have suffered wounds that would have killed a normal human three times over." Jones leaned forward, his single eye gleaming in the dim light of the cabin like a polished stone. "And I swore that one day I would make my sire pay for the cruelty he had shown my mother. And I made good on that oath the spring of 1844, when I tracked him and his latest brood mare to the wilds of Texas. It wasn't hard. He'd been preying on a few of the Spanish ranchers in the area. They were more than ready to believe it was the work of *lobo hombre*, especially if it happened to be a gringo.

"Howler thought he could come to this country and lose himself, escape his past. I made the bastard pay. Pay with his hide. Pay with his woman. He would have paid with his son, but I somehow managed to overlook you that day. But, in a way, I have taken as much pleasure in tormenting you, younger brother, as I did in skinning our sire alive."

"Why? What harm have I ever done you that would justify what you did to my wife and child?"

The sardonic smile disappeared from Jones' face. "What have you done? You have friends. You have family. You have people who love you and admire you. Me, I've never had a friend in my life. I'm too much of an outsider—normal humans can tell I'm trouble just by looking at me. And as for women—I can't get it up unless I hurt `em—or worse. The way I see it, if I can't have what you got—I'll make sure you can't have it, either."

As I listened to this failed monster drone on and one about the unfairness of his life, the rage I'd harbored for so many years stirred deep in my gut, twisting like a knife.

"Is that *it*?" I hissed. "Is that the sole reason you slaughtered my family like you would a buffalo cow and her calf? Because you're *jealous* of me?"

"You're seeing this all wrong, brother. Things like us, we aren't meant to be husbands and fathers. Besides, I did you favor. That whelp of yours was *esau*. He must of been, sporting all that hair. He wouldn't have amounted to much." Jones picked up the empty tin plate in front of Clubfoot Charley and went to the stove, ladling brown, savory stew onto it. I was salivating despite myself. Jones set the plate down on the table and pushed it in my direction.

"Here, to show you I don't mean you any ill-will, I'll share my grub with you. You know must be hungry after all this time..."

I *was* starving. And I don't mean it figuratively. The initial adrenalin rush from confronting Witchfinder Jones had blunted my hunger, but now the smell of the stew was making my gut rumble and my mouth fill with water. Without even thinking, I reached out and drew the plate towards me. There was something peculiar amongst the lumps of meat, carrots, potatoes, and onions.

It was an eye.

My wife's eye.

"What's the matter, Billy?" Jones leered at me from his side of the table. "She was good enough for you live—ain't she good enough for you dead?"

With a roar of anger, I overturned the table. My roar grew longer, higher; become a howl as the knot of hatred and rage and guilt inside me unravelled, wrapping my body in the painful joy of the change. Witchfinder Jones was on his feet, his revolver free of its holster. Even though I knew it was loaded with silver bullets, I did not care. It did not matter to me if I died in that lonely, snowbound mountain cabin. What did I have to live for, anyway? My wife and child were dead. My friends were dead. All I had known as a boy had been swept away in a cloud of gunsmoke, dust, and lies. I had nothing to lose. And all I wanted in the world at that precise moment was to tear my half-brother to shreds with my bare hands.

The first shot went wild. The second one went through my right side, just above the hip. The pain was immense, but such things no longer meant anything to me. When I struck Witchfinder it was like running into a solid wall of muscle and bone. I had never experienced anything like it before, and I'd brought down grown buffalo in my time.

He seemed surprised that I was still on my feet, so I used his confusion to my advantage, digging my talons into his wrist, forcing him to let go of the gun. Swearing in a language I did not know, he grabbed for the knife sheath on his belt. I leapt back just in time to see the silver blade cut an arc through the air where my throat had been only a second earlier.

"I don't know why those silver bullets didn't drop you, and I don't care! I'm going to take real pleasure in gutting you, brother," he snarled through bloodied lips. "I think I'll turn you into a pair of boots. Maybe a nice fur hat."

"Go ahead and kill me," I replied. "I don't care if I die. But I'm going to drag you to hell by the scruff of the neck like the sorry half-breed cur you are!"

Witchfinder's face crumpled inward, as if I'd somehow dealt him a painful blow, then bellowed like an angered bull and charged me, knocking me backward, into the pot-bellied stove. The stove tipped backwards, disconnecting it from the flue and scattering red-hot embers in every direction. Clubfoot Charley's cabin was small and cluttered. There were bundles of oily rags and everywhere. Within moments the cabin was ablaze.

Witchfinder came at me with the knife again, roaring wordlessly. His face was distorted by a bloodlust that was beyond anything I had ever seen in a human. He was in the grip of a fearsome animal rage that knew no mercy, gave no quarter. And that suited me just fine.

We circled one another in the middle of the burning cabin, growling like wild beasts, looking for the first sign of weakness in order to attack. Jones made the first move, lunging at me with his knife. I surged forward to meet him, grabbing his hand and twisting it one-hundred and eighty degrees, while driving the talons of my other hand into his face.

Jones screamed as his forearm shattered like a green branch. He dropped to his knees, his face a mess of blood and lacerations. His dead eye lay against his cheek like a limp dick. I twisted his arm again, turning it almost completely around in its socket.

"You're real good at killin' when you've got yourself up a posse of Mexicans or Mormons or whoever the hell you can talk into hirin' you, ain't you? And you're real good at killin' from a distance—or butcherin' helpless women and children. But when it comes to fightin' one-on-one with a full-blooded *vargr* you ain't nothin' but a sorry sack of shit! Our father was right to shun you—you're nothing but a mad dog!"

Witchfinder looked up at me with his remaining eye and spat a bloody wad of saliva that struck me square on the chest. "Fuck that shit. I'm just like you, Billy—except I wear the same skin all the time!"

"The hell you are!"

Just then Jones went for his fallen knife, with his good hand but he was too slow. I snatched it up and plunged it up to the hilt in his empty eye-socket, twisting it a full turn. Although this would have killed a normal human right on the spot, Jones's *vargr* heritage gave him the strength to lurch to his feet, clawing at the knife-hilt jutting out of his head. He knocked me down as he blundered blindly around the burning cabin, screaming at the top of his lungs.

As I moved to tackle him and tear out his throat, there was a loud sound and the roof collapsed, burying me under burning rafters and a ton of snow.

I'm uncertain as to how long I remained buried under the remains of Clubfoot Charley's cabin. While I was unconscious I was visited by a number of friends and family. All of them dead. First there was Sitting Bull, who looked in far better shape than when I last saw him. He was travelling in the company of Medicine Dog. I really wasn't surprised they'd hit it off in the Spirit World.

"Medicine Dog told me of how you tried to help me," my friend said. "Perhaps you could have changed things. Perhaps not. I appreciate the effort, though."

"Am I dead, uncle?"

"No. Not for good, anyway."

Someone touched Sitting Bull on the shoulder and he moved aside, allowing them to come forward. It was Digging Woman. Beside her stood our children, Small Wolf and Wolf Legs, holding hands. Although Small Wolf was the elder of the two, he looked to be half his younger brother's age.

"I bring you a gift, my husband," she smiled, lifting her right hand. Six glittering silver bullets fell onto the snow. "While you confronted my killer, I used my spirit-self to exchange his bullets with those of common lead."

I struggled to speak, but every breath I took made my ribcage feel as if it was trapped in a vise. "Digging Woman—I'm sorry—I'm sorry I wasn't there to protect you—to save you—I failed you—"

"Yes. That is true. But I still love you, Walking Wolf." She reached out to smooth my pelt, as she had often done as we lay curled together under our buffalo robes, but her hand had no weight and passed through me, making my skin tingle the way a leg does when it falls asleep. "I must go, my husband."

"Don't go—stay—stay with me—don't leave me alone—"

Digging Woman smiled and suddenly she was as young as when we first met. "I will love you forever, Walking Wolf. In this life—and all that follow."

"Digging Woman—no—" I raised my hand in a feeble attempt to grab her ghost and make her stay, but it was no use. She was gone. In her place were two shadowy, indistinct figures that moved just outside my field of vision. One stood upright, while the other seemed almost to move on all fours. They seemed uncertain—hesitant—then one that stood upright stepped forward, kneeling beside me. It was a woman, her hair the color of gold, her scent warm and familiar. I lifted my head and tried to get a better look, but her features remained fuzzy and indistinct.

"Mama?"

The second figure made a snuffling noise and my mother reluctantly pulled away, following my father into the dim haze of the afterlife.

When I woke up it was to the sound of something digging at the snow covering me. I was pinned under a charred rafter, my pelt was scorched, I had more broken ribs than whole ones, and there was a bullet in my hip, but outside of those injuries, I was relatively unscathed. Opening my eyes, I found myself muzzle-to-muzzle with a lone timber wolf. When I groaned and moved, it danced away, watching me warily from a safe distance as I climbed out of my frozen tomb. The timber wolf, recognizing me as being an unnatural thing, quickly quit the scene.

After extricating myself, I started digging out the ruins of the cabin.

I did not find Witchfinder Jones' body, nor did I find the shirt made of our father's pelt. However, I did manage to locate the tobacco pouch that had once been my mother's left teat. I also found six silver bullets laid side-by-side in the snow.

EPILOGUE

I took what was left of my ma and, come the spring thaw, I cremated it along with Digging Woman and Wolf Legs. I spent the rest of that winter in my true-skin, fending for myself as best I could, shunning all company, human or otherwise. During that long, cold, lonesome season I traveled so deep into grief and madness I came out the other side. The world I once knew no longer existed. Hell, it'd begun to disappear long before Sitting Bull's murder. In many ways I had still been innocent—if not in deed, then at least in spirit. But after Digging Woman's death, I was a changed man. Or werewolf, if you would.

Once I saw to it my loved ones got a proper send off into the Spirit World, I left that part of the country for good. With my friends and family dead, there was no reason for me to hang around, so I struck out west. I eventually made my way to California, and I eventually settled in the San Fernando Valley. Truth to tell, I own a good chunk of it, under various names and holding companies. No one would ever guess my wealth by looking at me or my house. I live modestly—some would even say austerely. I've discovered it pays to keep a low profile when one does not appear to age. But, then, the area's penchant for plastic surgery has provided me with camouflage for the last few decades.

I stand still as the years race pass, like a rock in the middle of a swift-running stream. I have seen fortunes made and lost—dynasties rise and fall. I've watched the White Man's magic expand beyond all known boundaries. Electricity. Antibiotics. Moonflights. Genetic engineering. Atomic energy. Indoor plumbing. I still don't trust them, of course. They're all still crazy. Maybe even crazier than before.

As for other *vargr*... I have made it a point to avoid them. They suffer from the same madness that afflicts the Whites. Not surprising, considering they are from the same world.

As for Witchfinder Jones: I do not doubt that my elder brother survived the battle in Clubfoot Charley's cabin. If he'd crawled away to die, I would have found him.

Although it's hard to imagine anyone taking such a wound and surviving, my brother is an uniquely tough individual. As much as I still hate his guts, I can't deny him that.

I suspect he managed to hole up somewhere after the fight and nurse himself back to health. But what would have been left of him after having his frontal lobes chopped into mincemeat? Is he able to remember who he is or—more importantly—*what* he is? Is he still an infernal engine of retribution, hunting down the monsters he so envies? Or is he drooling in his beard on a street corner somewhere, destined to an eternity of selling pencils? Or is he finally at peace with himself and settled down with a family of his own?

It's been one hundred and five years since we last met. I have yet to catch sign of him, although I have had ample opportunity to witness the atrocities of others of his misbegotten clan. Hitler, Manson, Dahmer, Rifkin... This century had been rife with the bloody misdeeds of the *esau*. And even though I have not seen or heard of him in over a century, I still keep an ear cocked for the sound of his tread on my porch. Creatures such as my brother do not give up the hunt lightly. Nor do they forgive.

Maybe its time I went out looking for him. Sitting down and writing out all the things that happened to me as a boy has made me nostalgic for the open spaces I once knew. It's been a long time since I wandered the countryside as I did as an youth. Digging Woman's newest incarnation is only six years old. It'll be another fifteen or twenty years before I can properly reintroduce myself to my wife. (We've been married twice since her death in 1890.) I've got the time, the opportunity, and the money to wander if I like. Yes, the more I think about it, the more I like it. It is time for Walking Wolf to stride the plains again.

What will I do if I find my long-lost brother, you ask?

Will I forgive him his trespasses and embrace him as my only living blood kin? Or will I show him the same mercy he gave my wife and child? And there *is* the matter of our father's pelt to be resolved. So, what will I do?

I ask you, dear reader; am I my brother's keeper?